# MEET THE GIRL TAL~

*Sabrina Wells* is petite, with curly auburn hair, sparkling hazel eyes, and a bubbly personality. Sabrina loves magazines, shopping, sleepovers, and most of all, she loves talking to her best friends.

*Katie Campbell's* a straight-A student and super athlete. With her blond hair, blue eyes, and matching clothes, she's everyone's idea of little miss perfect. But Katie has a few surprises for everyone, including herself!

*Randy Zak* has just moved to Acorn Falls from New York City, and is she ever cool! With her 'radical' spiked haircut and her hip New York clothes, Randy teaches everyone just how much fun it is to be different.

*Allison Cloud* is a Native American Indian. Allison's super smart and really beautiful. But she has one major problem: she's thirteen years old, five foot seven, and still growing!

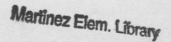

# Here's what they're talking about in
# Girl Talk

RANDY: I can't believe that you're actually going to model for *Belle*.

ALLISON: I can't believe it either.

RANDY: It's totally awesome! You must be really excited.

ALLISON: Well, maybe a little bit. But mostly I'm just plain nervous.

RANDY: Oh, come on! What have you got to worry about? Out of all the people *Belle* saw, they picked you – Allison Cloud.

ALLISON: Right! And that's exactly what I'm worried about.

## THE NEW YOU

### By L. E. Blair

GIRL TALK® series created by Western Publishing Company, Inc.

Produced by Angel Entertainment, Inc.

**Western Publishing Company, Inc., Racine, Wisconsin 53404**

Text by B. B. Calhoun

## Chapter One

"Okay, are you ready for this?" Sabrina asked, smiling. "You are absolutely going to freak out when you see this." She ran across the room to a stack of magazines near her bed. She began tossing them around frantically.

We all groaned. We were in Sabrina's attic bedroom for a sleepover. Sabrina had invited me — my name's Allison Cloud — and our friends Katie Campbell and Randy Zak to spend the night. We are all best friends and in the same seventh-grade homeroom at Bradley Junior High.

We groaned because Sabrina reads magazines constantly. She has subscriptions to at least four of them, and she buys tons of others. She reads them from cover to cover, and even cuts out her favorite pictures and tapes them up all over her room. Every week Sabs, that's one of her nicknames, has a crazy idea from

1

some magazine that she wants us to try.

Sabs finally found the magazine she was looking for and started flipping through the pages as fast as she could.

"Just hold on a sec. I had it earlier." Then she called out, "Here it is. I've found it. Wait until you hear this."

Randy faked a big yawn and fell down on the carpet pretending to be asleep from boredom. Even Katie rolled her eyes.

"Okay, here it is. Listen to this: *'Belle Magazine* wants *you!* Come be a part of our exciting American Beauties Search. We're traveling around the country, searching for America's natural beauty, and we're looking for *you*. Our special beauty experts can give you free personalized advice on hair, makeup, and clothes. They'll even give you a total makeover. Our photographers will be on hand, taking before-and-after photos, and you may end up modeling for *Belle*'s national American Beauties advertising campaign. Check listings below for the location nearest you.'"

Sabrina paused and looked at us very seriously.

"And here's the totally amazing part," she

announced dramatically. "It's happening this Saturday, October 16, at Widmere Mall. Can you believe our incredible luck?!"

"So, big deal," Randy said. "Why should we care?"

Sabs stared at her in disbelief. "Big deal? It's happening this Saturday, and the Widmere Mall is only twenty miles away. We're all going, and we're all going to get free makeovers, and maybe even get discovered and end up modeling for *Belle*. That's the big deal!"

"No way," Randy answered immediately. "I'm not giving up my Saturday to put on a lot of stupid outfits and let a bunch of turkeys mess up my hair and put junk all over my face."

"I don't think I'm really interested, either, Sabs," I said.

"Sounds a little embarrassing to me," said Katie.

"Well, I think you'll all change your minds when you hear this," Sabs replied. "You'll be dying to go after I read this to you. It's totally incredible."

She flipped through another magazine. "*Young Chic* horoscopes are the best, you know.

They're never wrong. Okay, Randy, you're Aries. Listen to this. *'The month may get off to a bad start, with past baggage weighing you down, but after the tenth comes your best time to make important decisions that could affect the rest of the year.'* Can you believe it? 'Past baggage weighing you down' — that's obviously about the tough time you had getting used to Acorn Falls at the beginning of the year, remember?"

Randy scowled. "Yeah, I remember, but it talks about the beginning of this month, which is October. That issue was for last month, in September."

Sabs wrinkled her forehead and looked down at the page. "Oh, yeah. Well, you probably had a little 'baggage' left over at the beginning of October. But the part about making an important decision is obviously about the makeover," Sabs replied.

"Listen to this, Katie. You're Virgo, right?" Sabs continued. *"'Don't be afraid of new ideas that come your way. The second half of the month is a good time to travel and make new contacts.'* Saturday is the sixteenth! That's the beginning of the second half of the month. It's a good time for you to travel to the Widmere Mall and

4

make new contacts. Pretty cool, huh?"

I started to say that going to the Widmere Mall wasn't exactly traveling, but Sabs looked really excited, and Katie was starting to smile, so I kept quiet.

"And Allison, wait till you hear yours. It's totally amazing. Here it is, Gemini. *'This is a good month for you, and you're in for a special blend of luck and adventure on the sixteenth, setting the tone for the weeks ahead. Be ready for it! Let go of the past; the new you is about to emerge.'* Al, it actually mentions the sixteenth! Can you believe it? Is that totally amazing, or what?"

"Here's mine, Pisces," continued Sabs breathlessly. *"'Lots of decisions and responsibilities are coming up in your life. Now's the time to move fast, but think carefully. You'll get lucky toward the middle of the month.'* All right, there it is. Mine says I'm supposed to make decisions, and I've made one. We're going to the makeover. And all our horoscopes said good things are going to happen to us sometime around the sixteenth. How much more evidence do you need?"

I could only imagine what my father, a lawyer, would say about that kind of "evidence." But all I said was "Forget it, Sabs."

"Oh, come on, you guys," she said, looking at the three of us. "You've got to be kidding me. How often do we get a chance like this?"

Randy was ready for her. "The whole thing sounds totally bogus to me. Everybody knows that all fashion models live in New York."

Sabs was exasperated. "That's not true, Randy," she said. "How do you think people get discovered?"

Randy just shrugged.

"I think it sounds like fun," said Katie suddenly.

"I don't know," said Randy. "I still don't trust this thing. They're probably just trying to get a bunch of magazine-heads like Sabrina to show up so that they can sell clothes and make-up."

Sabrina thought for a minute. "Okay, fine, we'll make a pact. We'll each bring just enough money for lunch. That way we won't be tempted to buy anything."

I didn't want to be mean, but I thought I had better point something out to everyone before they got carried away. "You know, I've been thinking. We're not the only people in Minnesota who have read about this. There are

6

probably going to be tons of girls there. *Belle* couldn't give everyone a free makeover if they opened a permanent stand in the Widmere Mall. You said yourself that it's only for one day."

Katie looked at me and nodded her head. She had a funny faraway look in her eyes. "It would be pretty neat to have our pictures in a magazine, though, wouldn't it?"

Sabrina was getting excited. "And even if we don't get our pictures taken, think of how much fun we would have being totally made over!"

"Even if we all wanted to go, which we don't, we'd have no way to get there," I pointed out.

"Oh, I've taken care of that," said Sabrina. "My brother Luke is going to drive us there and back. I just had to promise him one small favor."

We all groaned again. Sabs was forever getting one of her brothers to do something for her by promising to do a favor. Just last month she'd promised to wash her brother Mark's clothes for a month just to use his camera.

"What kind of favor, Sabs?" asked Randy.

"Well…" Sabrina bit her lip. "I have to wash his car every weekend for a month," she finally admitted.

"For a month!" Randy exclaimed.

"Well, now we really have to go since Sabs has to wash Luke's car every weekend for a month," said Katie. "Well, count me in," she announced. "I think it sounds like fun. I might come home looking gorgeous and shock everyone. And if I end up with my picture in a magazine, that would be so cool!"

"Great!" said Sabs.

Randy let out a whoop. "This I've got to see. I bet they're going to do all kinds of crazy things to you two."

Katie stood up and began pacing the room. "But what should I wear? What if they take pictures right there? What if they want you to be wearing *Belle* clothes?"

"Allison, you're coming, too, aren't you?" Sabrina implored.

I didn't know what to do. I was definitely not interested in getting made over. But I had the feeling that none of us would have to worry about makeovers with the amount of people who were going to show up. Anyway, I was pretty sure no one would be interested in taking pictures of an incredibly tall girl.

"I won't let them cut my hair, you know," said Katie. "I'm sure they try to convince people to cut their hair."

"I don't care what they do to me, as long as I look better," Sabs announced. "I wonder if I should go on a crash diet?"

"What do you say, Al? Are you coming along to watch the show?" Randy asked.

"Come on, Allison, it won't be any fun without you," said Katie.

"Of course you have to come with us," said Sabrina.

"Okay, I'll go," I said finally. *Besides*, I thought, *what could go wrong if I just went to watch?*

# Chapter Two

"Great," said Sabs. "Then we're all set."

"What happens at a makeover anyway?" I wondered out loud.

"I bet they tell you what kind of colors you should wear and what kind of clothes look good on you and stuff like that," said Katie.

"Do you think they would be willing to put a blue streak in my hair?" Randy asked, picking up a bottle of nail polish from Sabrina's dresser.

"I don't think so," I told her. I couldn't believe it. Now Randy was beginning to sound interested in this makeover business.

"Yeah," she said, smiling. "You're probably right, Al. They would never do anything so cool." Then she walked over to where I was sitting.

"Miss Cloud," Randy said in a really high voice. "I think that 'Autumn Gold' would be the perfect color for you." With that, she opened the bottle, grabbed my hand and started putting nail polish on my nails.

"Randy! Wait!" I protested. But it was too late. She had already started on a second fingernail.

Then Katie came over to get in the act. "Your hair, Miss Cloud, we must do something about your hair." She held up one of my braids and began tying it in a knot. I looked in the mirror on top of Sabrina's dresser and decided I didn't want to watch what else she was going to do.

"Your cheeks are much too pale, Miss Cloud," said Sabrina and she picked up a huge, fluffy, makeup brush and started brushing pink powder on my face. "A little blush will take care of that."

I pleaded with them, "Guys, don't you think that's enough?" They just laughed and shook their heads. Ten minutes later they let me look in the mirror. I took one look at my face and ran straight to the bathroom to wash off the makeup and fix my hair. Although I wasn't used to makeup and I thought they had put too much on, I had to admit I didn't look half bad.

When I came out of the bathroom, Sabs was lying across her bed with another magazine.

"I hope they make my hair over," she sighed. "Hey, look at this," she cried, suddenly sitting up on the bed. "Flour, water, and egg. It's supposed to restore body to dry and damaged hair and repair split ends."

Katie giggled. "It sounds like a cake recipe."

Sabrina jumped up. "Oh, let's do it. I really want to get my hair in shape before Saturday."

"It's a makeover, Sabrina. Your hair is not supposed to be in good shape."

"Oh, who cares?" said Sabrina. "I want to do it. If I go down to the kitchen and get the stuff, will one of you put it on my hair?"

"Sure, I'll do it, Sabs," Randy said with a grin. Twenty minutes later, Randy's hands and arms were white and gooey as she energetically kneaded the flour, water, and egg mixture in a big bowl. I couldn't help noticing that a lot of the flour was falling on Sabrina's rug.

When the mixture was ready, Randy spread it all over Sabs's head until it looked like a yellowish-white hood.

"Okay, Sabs, you're done," said Randy, laughing, "and I must say you look ravishing."

"Just wait and see what I look like after I rinse off this goo," Sabs answered.

"If it works, maybe I'll have you do it to me, too, Randy," said Katie excitedly.

"I'll be right back," said Sabrina, jumping up

and running downstairs to the bathroom.

A few minutes later Sabrina reappeared at the door. She was wearing her pink terry cloth bathrobe and she had a pink towel wrapped around her hair. She looked very upset.

"Didn't it work?" asked Katie.

Sabrina's lower lip began to tremble. "I can't get it out," she blurted.

Sure enough, when she unwrapped the towel, we saw hundreds of yellowish-white globs stuck all through her wet, tangled, red hair.

"Don't worry, Sabs, we'll get it out," Katie said. "Where's your comb?"

"Oh, what am I going to do?" Sabs moaned.

"It's okay," I told her. "We'll get it out."

We sat down on the rug in a circle around Sabrina. We each took a section of her hair and started to pick at the sticky globs.

"I'm really sorry, Sabs. I don't know what we did wrong," said Randy. She looked upset.

"No, problem, Sabs. We're going to get it all out. It just might take a little while," Katie said, pulling at Sabrina's hair with the comb.

"I just hope we get it all out by Saturday!" Sabrina wailed. She picked up the magazine and began to search the article on hair treatments.

Suddenly she let out a yelp. "Hey you guys, the recipe for the masque is continued on page 127. We only mixed up part of it! It was supposed to have a half a cup of olive oil and the juice of one lemon!"

"Oh, I see," I said quietly. "The olive oil would probably have made the mixture less sticky, and more... slippery. Basically, what we've made here is a kind of paste, or glue —"

"You mean it's stuck to my hair forever?!" Sabrina wailed.

"Not if we can figure out the right antidote. Like in science class, remember? Once, my brother Charlie got tar in his hair and my mother used peanut butter to get it out."

"Okay, so let's try it," said Randy hopefully.

"There's peanut butter in the kitchen," said Sabrina.

"I'll run and get it," volunteered Katie.

Just then, we heard a loud clumping sound on the stairs.

"Someone's on their way up here!" Sabs whispered frantically. "Quick, lock the door."

We all made a rush for it, but I got there first. I guess there are some good things about having long legs.

"Hey, what's going on?" asked Sam, Sabrina's twin brother. Then he shook the doorknob.

"Nothing at all," Sabrina called back, starting to snicker. That started Katie giggling, too.

"Well, Nick's here," said Sam. "and there's a really cool movie coming on TV called *Zombies from Planet Zena*." Nick is Sam's best friend.

"You look like a zombie from planet Zena," Katie whispered to Sabrina, and burst out laughing.

"What's so funny? What are you guys doing?" asked Sam.

I thought about explaining calmly to Nick and Sam that we were trying to get glue out of Sabrina's hair. Then I started laughing, too. We heard Sam mumble something in disgust and clump back down the stairs.

We all looked at each other and that made us laugh even harder. Soon we were holding our stomachs and tears were running down our cheeks.

When we finally managed to stop laughing we spent the next hour working on Sabrina's hair. We had to do it in secret because if Sam and Nick found out about Sabrina's sticky hair, everyone at Bradley Junior High would know about it on

Monday.

It took an entire jar of peanut butter to get the glue out of Sabrina's hair. We finished in time to join Sam and Nick in the Wells' TV room as they watched *Zombies from Planet Zena*. We didn't see the ending though. After a while, Sam and Nick kicked us all out of the room because we were laughing too much.

## Chapter Three

On Monday in English class, which is also our homeroom, it was my turn to read from *Tom Sawyer*. English happens to be my favorite subject, and I love our teacher, Ms. Staats. It's also the only class that Katie, Randy, Sabs, and I have together. Since it's right before lunch everyone gets restless. I finished reading and sat down. I glanced over at Katie, who sits next to me. She was doodling in her notebook, drawing a lot of hearts and flowers. Then the bell rang.

Suddenly everyone was wide awake, gathering their belongings and getting ready to leave. Ms. Staats put up her hand.

"Hold on a minute," she said. "I have one announcement."

A few kids sighed, not wanting to miss a minute of lunch.

Ms. Staats went on. "The year's first issue of *The Beacon*, Bradley Junior High's literary magazine, comes out in three weeks. I want all of you to think about submitting a story or a poem. The deadline is a week from Friday."

Everyone picked up their books and headed for the door.

"Thank goodness it's lunchtime. I'm starved," said Katie as she followed me down the aisle.

As we walked toward Ms. Staats's desk, she called me over. "Allison, hold on a minute, please. I'd like to speak to you."

"Allison, I really hope you'll write something for *The Beacon*," Ms. Staats said. "This is a perfect opportunity for you to share your writing talents with the rest of the school."

"Okay," I said, a little embarrassed. "I would like to submit something."

"Good, please start something soon. The deadline is a week from Friday. I'm looking forward to seeing what you come up with."

I practically skipped to the cafeteria. I was really excited, and I even had a few ideas already.

Katie was already sitting with Sabrina and Randy. I filled my tray and joined their table.

"Hi, Al," Katie said. "What did Ms. Staats want to talk to you about?"

"Oh, nothing really," I said, not wanting to

brag. "She just wanted to tell me —" I searched my mind for the right way to say it.

Just then, Stacy Hansen and her clones approached the table. Randy, Katie, Sabrina, and I call her Stacy the Great. Our two groups don't get along very well. Stacy never seems to do anything without her friends Eva Malone, B.Z. Latimer, and Laurel Spencer. They all act stuck-up but Stacy is the worst. She probably acts that way because her father, Mr. Hansen, is the principal of our school.

Stacy sighed loudly and looked around the cafeteria. "I can't believe this," she exclaimed. "There's nowhere to sit!"

They continued searching the room until their eyes came to rest at the empty spot at the end of our table. It was the only available place to sit in the whole cafeteria.

"Oh, let's just sit there," B.Z. said finally. "My arms are ready to fall off from carrying this tray." She looked in the direction of our table.

"Oh, I can't believe it," Eva moaned.

"First we miss most of lunch," said Stacy in a disgusted voice, "and now this." She flopped down at the exact spot farthest from where Sabrina, Katie, Randy, and I were sitting.

"Don't do us any favors," muttered Randy

under her breath.

"Come on, Randy, don't start anything," Katie whispered to her.

"Well, I guess I do have to eat," Eva said loudly, taking the seat across from Stacy. That was the cue for B.Z. and Laurel to sit down, too.

"Let's just pretend they're not here and go on talking as usual," Sabrina whispered. "So, Katie," she said more loudly, "what are you going to wear to Widmere on Saturday?"

Stacy turned and stared at us. Eva gasped. "Don't tell me all of you are going to the makeover on Saturday?!" she shrieked.

"How did *you* hear about it?" Sabrina asked defensively.

"Well, it's not that big a secret if you can read," Laurel pointed out.

"Are you guys going?" Katie asked.

"Well, of course," said Stacy. "This is a perfect opportunity for me. I've always wanted to model, you know."

"What makes you so sure you'll get picked?" Sabrina asked.

Stacy flipped her wavy, blond hair over her shoulder. "Oh, I think I have a pretty good chance," she said.

"Why, you guys can't possibly think that any of *you* could be picked, do you?" Eva sneered.

"I don't think any of us should expect to be picked," I said. "After all, Minnesota is a big state."

"Only if you think small," said Stacy.

"It must be pretty hard for Allison Cloud to do anything small," said Eva, snickering. I tried not to pay attention. I should be used to people saying things about how tall I am. But it still bothers me anyway.

Randy, who had been fuming silently, turned and faced Eva. "I can't imagine how anyone could manage to take a picture of you, Eva, since your mouth is always moving!"

Then the period bell rang. Thank goodness!

"Come on, Randy, it's time for science class," I said to her.

"Well, I can't say I'm sorry this lunch is over," Stacy said in a huff and picked up her tray.

"Really," said Eva.

I practically had to drag Randy all the way to the science lab. Randy and I are lab partners. This past month we had been testing the pH balance of different substances with litmus paper. We were supposed to write down a list of the alkaline substances and a list of the acid substances in our workbooks. It's a good thing I knew what we were doing, because Randy was still mad and not really paying attention.

It didn't help that Laurel and Eva are in the same science class, and kept looking at us and whispering. Somehow, though, it was easier for me to stay calm than it was for Randy. I didn't see why we should let them get to us. And it was silly to argue about what might happen at the makeover. We would all find out on Saturday, anyway. When you think about it, I guess you could say that Randy has more of an acid personality, while mine is more alkaline.

# Chapter Four

For some reason, I had a really hard time getting dressed on the day of the makeover. It wasn't that I cared about what I wore or anything, but I was having one of those mornings when nothing felt comfortable. In the end, I wore jeans and a sweater, my old standby, and at the last minute I tied a white ribbon around my braid.

When I was ready to leave I looked around my room to make sure that everything was nice and neat. My room is my favorite place in the whole house. My father and I painted it together a couple of years ago. The walls are all cream colored with a stripe of rust red and a stripe of chocolate brown all around the top near the ceiling. I picked those colors because they go with the big rag rug that my grandmother made for me. My bed has a big comforter in the same colors and there are matching curtains on the windows.

There's a big mahogany chest of drawers in

one corner and an old-fashioned rolltop desk in another. On both sides of the door, there are two huge floor-to-ceiling bookcases, absolutely filled with books. The absolutely best part of my room is the window seat. I think the window seat is special to me because that's where I sit and write my poetry. It's covered with rust red cushions and I keep special books and pictures inside. My favorite picture is one of Charlie and me sitting on the hood of our car during our last vacation.

I felt satisfied that my room was perfect so I headed for Sabrina's house. Everyone was waiting in the driveway. Luke was leaning against his car, looking bored.

"Glad you made it, Al," said Randy with a grin. "These two are about to drive me nuts. They've been running upstairs and changing their clothes every five minutes."

"I wouldn't talk, Randy," Sabs teased. "You look pretty decked out yourself, if you ask me."

I looked at Randy. Something seemed different. In addition to her usual black jeans and black bomber jacket she was wearing a zebra-striped T-shirt. She also had on pointy purple, suede ankle boots that I had never seen before.

"Hey, let's get moving," said Luke. "I don't

have all day, you know." We all piled into the car. Sabs got in the front seat next to her brother and Katie squashed in between Randy and me in the back.

"Oh, I almost forgot!" Sabrina said as we pulled out of the driveway. She twisted around and leaned over the front seat. "My dad just ordered a bunch of neat tapes from a videotape club he joined. He said we could look at the tapes anytime we want. Why don't you guys come over Thursday right after school and we'll pick out a movie. Mom said she'll watch with us and we can make popcorn balls."

"Wow!" said Katie. "I love watching movies after school. Did your dad order any music videos?"

"Do you have any horror movies?" asked Randy, who loves horror movies with a passion. "That will be great! Your mom's popcorn balls are the best."

"I'm sure it will be okay with my mom," I told Sabs. "I'll be there, too."

Luke pulled up in front of the main entrance and let us out, telling us he'd be back at three o'clock to pick us up.

As soon as we walked into the mall, we saw a

big banner that said, "Widmere Welcomes *Belle Magazine*'s American Beauties Search!" A smaller sign said, "Makeover participants, follow blue arrows." My stomach jumped a little.

"Well, I guess we're here on the right day," Randy said.

"Oh, I'm so unbelievably nervous," Katie added.

"Isn't this incredibly exciting?" said Sabrina, clutching my arm.

As we followed the trail of blue arrows through the mall, I kept looking for other girls on their way to a makeover. I really didn't see any, and I began to think that maybe I had been wrong about all the people who were going to show up for this thing. I also couldn't seem to get my stomach to calm down.

Then the path of blue arrows led us toward a set of big, steel double doors. A small sign taped to one of the doors said, "Makeover participants, this way." We looked at each other, shrugged, and pushed. Suddenly, we were back outside in what looked like a parking lot, and we were surrounded by hundreds of people!

I looked around. I had never seen so many girls my age in one place before. There must have been five hundred of them!

"What a total scene," said Randy, stunned.

"Oh, my gosh, this is unbelievable," said Katie. "Look at all these people. We'll never get in!"

"We'll find a way in," Sabs said confidently. "We have to. We came all this way." She turned to me. "Al, can you see anything up there?"

I'm used to this. At five foot seven, I often get asked to check out what's going on above the crowd.

But there were just too many people, and I couldn't see a thing.

"We have to come up with a plan of action," Sabrina said.

"But what?" Katie asked hopelessly.

Just then Randy let out a moan. "Oh, great," she said.

"What's the matter?" Katie asked her.

"See for yourself," said Randy.

We looked in the direction Randy was pointing and we saw Stacy, Eva, B.Z., and Laurel. B.Z. was craning her neck, trying to see above the crowd. Laurel looked bored, and Eva was putting on lip gloss. Stacy was facing away from us and was bent over at the waist vigorously brushing the underside of her hair.

"Quick, let's move to another spot before they see us," said Katie.

"Are you kidding? And pass up an easy target like that?" asked Randy, gesturing toward Stacy.

"Randy, if you start anything and get us kicked out of here, I'll kill you," Sabrina warned.

"I think we can get a better view of the front from over there," I said, leading Randy away from Stacy and her group.

Suddenly a woman started talking through a bullhorn.

"Good afternoon everyone, and welcome to *Belle Magazine*'s American Beauties Search!" the woman said.

A cheer went up from the crowd. My stomach did a quick flip-flop.

"There are five Belle representatives up here. Each of them is holding a helium balloon. Please form one line in front of each of the five people with the balloons."

The crowd started to move.

"Okay," Sabrina whispered, "here's the plan. When we get up there, we each join a different line. That way we can have everything covered."

"But there are five lines, and only four of us," I

reminded her.

"Well, the odds will still be with us," she answered. "Besides, we have the stars on our side. Remember the horoscopes!"

What Sabrina didn't seem to realize was that even if there was anything to those horoscope predictions, the odds wouldn't really be with us unless we were the only Pisces, Virgo, Aries, and Gemini in the crowd.

As we made our way toward the front, I saw the five people with the balloons. They were standing in front of an area near the building that had been roped off. Each person was holding a balloon of a different color. Beside each person was a big plastic garbage pail. As the girls on each line approached the people with the balloons, they reached into the pails and pulled out little plastic tote bags that said *Belle* on them.

"Okay, get ready," Sabs instructed us.

Then I saw the woman with the yellow balloon give a girl a little red ticket instead of a bag.

"Please step this way," she said, directing the girl behind the velvet rope and toward a small glass door in the building behind her.

Katie noticed, too. "Look," she said, "that girl got in. They gave her a special ticket."

"I'm going on that line," Sabrina said quickly. She hurried over to the right.

Katie looked disappointed. "Do we still have to spread out?" she asked.

"Katie, I'm sure that's not the only line where they're giving out those tickets," I told her. "Otherwise, everyone would have figured it out by now, and they'd all be standing on that line. Sabs is probably right. We should spread out." I looked around. "See, the man with the purple balloon just gave that girl one, too," I said, pointing out a girl who was heading for the glass door.

Katie jumped. "I'm going on that line," she said happily, and ran off to join the line next to Sabrina's.

Randy joined the line in front of a woman with a green balloon. That left me with a choice between the woman with a blue balloon or the man with a white one. I joined the woman's line because it was next to Randy's.

After watching for a moment, I began to realize that there was some kind of pattern to the way they were handing out those red tickets. They didn't give them out very often, but they seemed to do so at regular intervals. My father says that if you pay attention to any pattern long enough, you'll figure it out eventually.

Randy's line was on my right. I decided to count her line to see how many girls were given bags before the next ticket was handed out. Nine. Nine girls got bags and the tenth one got a ticket. I looked to my left, at the line in front of the man with the white balloon. I waited until a ticket was given out and started counting. Number ten got the ticket again!

I starting counting Randy's line again. But this time, fourteen people got bags, and then the fifteenth person got a ticket. Maybe there wasn't a pattern, after all.

I looked at the line to my left. Again, fourteen people got bags, and the fifteenth person got a red ticket.

Back on Randy's line, she was the ninth person on line after the last red ticket. I watched as she stepped up to the woman with the green balloon and was given a bag, and then as the girl behind her — number ten — got a ticket! So that was the pattern: first every tenth girl got a ticket, then every fifteenth girl got one, and then back to ten, and so on.

I realized that I could test my theory if I joined the line to my left. According to my calculations, I would be number ten. I hurried over, counting the people ahead of me. The line moved ahead. The two people ahead of me were given bags. As I stepped up to the man with the white balloon, he winked and handed me a red ticket. I was right!

"Okay, doll, you're one of the lucky ones," he said, smiling. "Go right through that glass door. Have fun!" Then I realized what I had done. I had solved the ticket pattern, but now they thought I wanted to have a makeover!

## Chapter Five

I looked around frantically. I had to explain to someone right away that there had been a mistake. My eye caught Sabrina waving to me wildly from the crowd.

"Allison, you did it! You're in!" she called out.

I rushed over to where she was standing. But when I got near the rope, the woman with the yellow balloon stopped me.

I looked pleadingly at Sabrina and said, "You have to get me out of here!"

"Are you kidding?" she asked with amazement. "This is great! You actually got in!"

Then I saw Randy and Katie making their way toward us. Katie was grinning, and Randy was giving me the thumbs-up signal.

"Totally excellent!" Randy yelled when she got within hearing distance.

Katie did her best to hug me over the rope. "Oh, Allison! This is wonderful, I'm so happy for you!" she squealed.

"Hold on a minute, everybody," I said firmly. "I don't want a makeover. I'm not going in there." I looked back at the woman with the yellow balloon.

"But you have to, Al," Sabs whined. "You're the only one of us who got in!"

"Besides," Katie added, "wait till you hear who else got in — Stacy and B.Z.!!"

They all looked at me. "Please Allison, you really have to go!" said Sabs. "After all those things they said to us! We have to prove to them that they're not the only ones who could get in."

"I hate to say it, Al, but we've got to show them. Come on, you can do it!" said Randy, tapping my shoulder.

"Then one of *you* go in!" I answered, and turned immediately to the woman with the yellow balloon. "Excuse me," I said, "but I'd like to give my ticket to one of my friends."

"No switching allowed," she said. "You girls will have to clear this area now."

"Go get 'em, Al!" Randy called.

"Good luck!" said Katie.

"We'll meet you around the other side!" Sabs promised.

I sighed and turned toward the glass door. I found myself in a hallway and was greeted by a tall woman wearing glasses and holding a clipboard. She was standing next to a big table that was covered with stacks of sweatshirts and hats.

"Hi, congratulations, and welcome to *Belle*," she said cheerfully, taking my ticket and handing me a sweatshirt and a hat. The sweatshirt was teal with the *Belle* logo in white on the front and the hat was white with the logo in teal. They looked really cool together.

"Don't be nervous. I'm sure you'll have a great time. Go right in there," she said. "Have fun!"

I walked through the second door and into a big room. There were about fifty girls sitting on folding chairs, all with sweatshirts and hats in their laps. A tiny woman with straight black hair and bangs stood at the front of the room. I walked around and sat near the back of the room.

"Good afternoon, everyone. My name is Darla Jones. Please fill out these forms with your name, age, address, telephone number, parents' names, and how you heard about the *Belle* American Beauties Search," said Darla Jones. A girl in the row in front of me turned around and passed me a box of little pencils. I filled in all the information. When I got to the part about how I had heard about the makeovers, I was tempted to answer, "I was talked into coming by a magazine maniac." But instead I just wrote down, "from a magazine."

"Now, we're going to divide you into groups. One group will go with David, our hairstylist, for a hair clinic." A man with shoulder-length hair stood up and waved to us. "Another group will go with Candy, our makeup artist. She will run the makeup clinic." A woman with very short blond hair stood up for a moment. "And the third group will go with Maryann. She's our fashion expert and she's going to explain how to put together a great look with *Belle* fashions and accessories." Maryann, the tall woman who had passed out sweatshirts and forms, stood up and smiled.

"Oh, yes," Darla went on, "I'm *Belle*'s modeling representative here today. So, let's take a break and have a light snack, while we assign you to your groups. Then I'll come around and collect your forms."

Someone passed around fruit, cookies, and juice. I was glad they thought of food because I was starving. I hadn't eaten anything since breakfast, and it had to be nearly one o'clock by now.

Suddenly I heard an unpleasantly familiar laugh. I looked over and saw Stacy Hansen and B.Z. Latimer.

"What happened, Allison?" Stacy asked. "Did you go through the wrong door?"

Before I had a chance to answer Stacy, a big flash of light went off to my left. I looked over and saw Darla Jones with a Polaroid camera. She was surrounded by the hairdresser, the makeup lady, and the tall woman named Maryann. Darla was talking to a little blond girl whose picture she had just taken. She clipped the picture to the girl's form, put the form in a folder she was carrying, and started to walk straight toward me.

"Hello," said Darla, taking my form and glancing at it. "Allison, would you please stand up for me?"

This was the moment I had been dreading. This woman was so tiny and petite, I just knew I would look like Godzilla standing in front of her. Since I didn't have much choice, I stood up.

Darla Jones's face brightened. "Wonderful!" she said. "How tall are you, Allison?"

"Five seven," I admitted. This was really embarrassing. I couldn't imagine what she thought was so wonderful about towering above almost everyone you knew.

Maryann smiled at me. "Try to relax, Allison. Just stand up straight."

I really wanted to crawl under a chair and hide until the whole thing was over and everyone was gone. But I could tell that Maryann was doing her best to make me feel better, so I straightened up a little bit and tried to smile.

Darla turned to the man with the shoulder-length hair. "Well, David?"

"Let me take a look at your hair, honey," he said to me. I turned around and showed him my braid.

"Very nice, very long," he commented. "Let's see here." Before I knew it, he had pulled off the ribbon and rubber band from my braid, and had loosened my hair. "Magnificent! So thick!" he said, running his hands through my hair.

This was unbelievable. First I had to announce my height in front of all of them, and now some strange man was making a mess of my hair! I turned back to them, and I could feel my face burning with embarrassment.

Candy, the makeup artist, reached toward me. "Excellent skin," she said. "She doesn't need much makeup."

"Such beautiful, thick hair!" exclaimed David, flipping all of my hair from one side of my face to the other. "And the color! Jet black! I love it!" he announced.

"Yes," said Darla thoughtfully, looking down at my form. "Allison Cloud," she said. "Cloud... are you a Native American, Allison?"

"Yes. My family is Chippewa," I told her.

Before I knew what was happening, there was a flash of light; Darla Jones had taken my picture. This was sure to be the worst possible picture of me in existence. My hair was totally messed up, and I was probably squinting and blinking from the flash. Plus the picture had been taken by someone a foot shorter than me who probably had a great view of the underside of my chin.

Well, one thing was for sure, I wouldn't have to worry about how to get out of there. As soon as they saw the picture, they would probably show me straight to the door. The funny thing is, now I kind of wanted to stay and go through with it.

"Can I have your attention, please!" Darla called out. "Will the following girls please go with David to the hair clinic."

My name wasn't called, and I was very

relieved. Who knows what that guy David would have done to me if I had let him near my hair again.

Then Darla read out the names of the people who were supposed to go with Candy to the makeup clinic. I still didn't hear my name, but I did notice that B.Z. Latimer was called.

Finally, Darla read the names of the people who were supposed to go with Maryann. I was pretty surprised when my name wasn't announced for that group, either. Maybe there had been some kind of mistake, or maybe this was their way of telling me that they wanted me to leave. Darla had probably gotten a good look at my picture.

"I have one final announcement," Darla said. "Will the following girls please see me for a minute before we start." She looked down at the list in front of her and read off names: "Kelly Kay O'Connor, Suzi Kim, Keisha Lewis, Stacy Hansen, and Allison Cloud."

I looked around and wondered what Darla Jones wanted. I figured she was going to kick me out — but Stacy, too? I couldn't believe it. I joined the other four girls near Darla Jones. Even though there were only five of us, Stacy managed to act as if she didn't know I was there. She was busy smiling and batting her eyes at Darla Jones.

"I wanted to speak with each of you for a few minutes before sending you to one of the makeover clinics," Darla began. "We may be interested in using you in the American Beauties campaign."

A couple of the girls gasped. Stacy smiled even harder. Darla went on. "We're trying to show that beauty in America comes in many varieties, and I think that's pretty clear, looking at all of you."

I looked around. It was true. We were all very different looking. One girl had long, wavy red hair, very pale skin, and these really light green eyes. Another girl was Asian with straight, silky black hair that came to just above her shoulders. The third girl was Black, with dark brown hair and really huge brown eyes. I couldn't help noticing that she was at least as tall as I was. Of course there was also blond, brown-eyed Stacy, and me with my long, black hair and darkish complexion. We made a pretty unusual-looking group.

"I've got all of your forms and if we decide to use you, you'll be hearing from us. Now Maryann will read off which group you are to join."

Well that was that. I was certain that I'd never hear from *Belle Magazine* again. Part of me felt disappointed, though, that they wouldn't tell us right then and there what was going to happen.

Fortunately, I got to go to Maryann's workshop on clothes and accessories. I was glad that Stacy went to the makeup workshop to join B.Z. I didn't feel like being with them. I was sure they'd try to do something to embarrass me.

To my surprise the clothing workshop was pretty interesting. I learned that I look best in bright, intense colors, which isn't the case for many people.

When it was all over , I stood up and tried to collect all the forms, booklets, samples, and of course the sweatshirt and hat they had given us. Suddenly, I heard a voice behind me. "So, is this your first job?"

I turned around and saw the redheaded girl.

"Job?" I asked her.

"Yeah, modeling," she answered. "Although they're probably not going to pay us, since it was just a search. My mom will be happy anyway, though."

"Your mom? Did she come for a makeover?"

"No," she said and laughed. "But she's dying

for me to make it in modeling or show business."

"I have a friend she should meet," I joked, thinking of Sabs.

Then I remembered — Sabs! Her brother Luke was supposed to meet us all at three.

I turned quickly to the girl. "Do you know what time it is?" I asked.

"Sure," she answered, looking down at her watch. "It's three nineteen exactly."

I couldn't believe it was that late. What if I had missed them?

"Oh, my gosh, I've got to go," I said. "I'm really late and my friends are waiting!"

"Okay, bye," she said. "I hope I'll see you if they call us for the same thing."

"Yeah, I guess," I answered, running toward the door.

"Hey, what's your name?" she called after me.

"Allison. Allison Cloud," I called back.

"Okay Allison, I'm Kelly Kay. Actually I'm Kelly O'Connor, but my middle name is Kay. My mother says I should use Kelly Kay. She says it sounds nicer — more professional or something. See you!"

I thought it was pretty funny that Kelly's own mother didn't want her to use her real full name. I waved good-bye quickly and hurried out of the room. I ran down the hall, through the double doors, and out into the mall.

I saw Katie, Randy, and Sabrina sitting on a bench next to a planter and holding their little plastic bags from *Belle*. As soon as they saw me, they jumped up and ran toward me eagerly.

They had a million questions.

I tried my best to explain about Darla Jones, Stacy and B.Z., David the hairdresser, and everything that had happened. Meanwhile, Sabs hurried us all out the door to her brother's car.

It turned out that inside each *Belle* tote bag was a *Belle* T-shirt, a fruit-flavored lip gloss, and a catalog of *Belle* clothes.

Sabrina, Katie, and Randy couldn't stop talking about what had happened. They seemed to think I was practically famous already. I pointed out that I wasn't even sure if Darla Jones would ever call me, but they seemed sure that she would. What I didn't tell them was that I still wasn't sure if I *wanted* Darla Jones to call me.

## Chapter Six

By Sunday night, I had truly convinced myself that I would never hear from *Belle* or Darla Jones again. I still hadn't told my parents anything about the makeover. It wasn't a big secret; it's just that every time something happens to someone in our family, we get together and talk about it for what seems like hours. Since I didn't think anything was going to happen, I didn't see any reason to get my family started in on one of their big discussions.

The next day, school went by quickly. When I got to my locker after the last class of the day, Sabs, Randy, and Katie were waiting for me. To my surprise Stacy was standing there, too.

Stacy started talking before anyone else had a chance. "So, Allison," she said sweetly, "have you heard from *Belle* yet?"

"No," I said quickly.

"That's too bad. Well, I've heard from them.

My mother told my father that they called at lunchtime," she replied with a toss of her blond hair. "I guess I'll just have to be the only girl from Acorn Falls to make it." Then she flashed a smile and walked away.

"Don't worry," Sabs said. "Stacy's only trying to upset you."

"Please just forget about *Belle*," I pleaded, cutting her off. "I never thought they would call."

"Don't be silly!" Sabs exclaimed, looking shocked. "Of course they're going to call. And I'll bet they'll even put your picture on the cover of the magazine. Stacy doesn't know what she's talking about."

"Sabs, they can't put anything on the cover of a magazine. It's only an advertising campaign," I pointed out. "When was the last time you ever saw an ad on the cover of a magazine?"

"Well, knowing Stacy, she'll manage to push herself onto the cover of something," said Katie.

Randy made a face. "Ugh! I can't believe they called her. Now I'm sure they'll call you. You're so much prettier."

"Come on, Al, we're going down to Fitzie's for ice cream. Let's celebrate your future modeling career." Sabs looked at the others. "Our treat," she added.

"Oh, I don't think so," I said.

"Come on, Al, a little hot fudge will do you good," Randy put in.

"No, really, guys, I'm so tired. I just want to go home."

"Okay," said Sabs, "but we're only going to let you get out of it if you promise that you're really going to go home and get some beauty sleep."

"Yeah," said Randy, "we don't want you to fall asleep during the photo session."

Katie looked disappointed. "Feel better, Al, and don't worry about dumb old Stacy and her cracks."

They walked me to the bike rack outside and we said good-bye. I was glad it was still warm enough to ride my bike to and from school. In a few weeks it would start getting cold, and then I would have to get a ride with my father or take the school bus.

As soon as I got home, I knew something was up. My mother was sitting at the kitchen table, waiting for me, with a little piece of paper in front of her.

"Hi, Allison. Come and sit down at the table," she said. "I got a very interesting phone call about you today."

"Really?" I asked, putting my backpack on a chair and standing in front of the table.

"Someone named Darla Jones."

My heart skipped a beat. I couldn't believe it! I looked at my mother. I felt guilty. I knew she wasn't going to be very happy that I hadn't told her about the makeover.

"I don't understand why you didn't say anything to us," said Mom.

"I'm sorry, Mom."

"Listen, Allison, I want you to know that you don't have to feel embarrassed about wanting to go to a makeover, or a beauty search, or whatever it is. It's normal for a girl your age."

"But Mom, I —"

She went on. "I don't think there's anything wrong with your wanting to do a little modeling. I think this is a fine opportunity for you. I'm sure it sounds appealing and glamorous now, but you may discover that it's also very hard work."

"But Mom, that wasn't it," I said. "I just didn't think Darla Jones was really going to call me, or I would have told you, really, Mom."

"Well," she said, standing up and putting her arm on my shoulder, "you don't have to worry. I said yes."

What was she talking about? "Yes to what? What do you mean?" I asked her.

"Why, yes to your going to the shoot, or whatever it is they call it, tomorrow," she explained.

"Mom, what are you talking about? What shoot tomorrow?" I demanded.

"Darla Jones said they want you for a shoot tomorrow in Widmere. She said she needed permission from a parent in order for you to go." Mom picked up the slip of paper from the table and looked at it. "I'm supposed to take you to the football field at Green Acres High School in Widmere. Now, she also mentioned that another girl from Acorn Falls is going...." She looked at the paper again. "Stacy Hansen. Isn't that Mr. Hansen's daughter? She's in seventh grade with you, isn't she?"

"She sure is," I answered, sitting down in a chair with a thump.

"Well, then, that's wonderful. Miss Jones asked if I would mind driving you and Stacy to Widmere tomorrow afternoon. I told her it would be a pleasure. Miss Jones also said that Mrs. Hansen will pick up the two of you when it's over and drive you back home."

I couldn't believe my ears. Not only was I supposed to pose for pictures with Stacy Hansen, but I had to ride all the way to Widmere and back with her, too.

My mother looked at me closely. "Is something wrong, Allison? You look worried."

"No, I'm okay," I answered.

"Are you worried about what your father will say about all of this? Because if that's it, you can relax. I've already talked to him. He eventually agreed that this might be a good learning experience for you."

"Great, Mom," I said. "Thanks." But I knew what that meant — it meant that she had talked him into it. He would never have agreed on his own to my doing something like this. He is very conservative.

At that moment, my little brother Charlie ran into the room carrying a long, plastic sword. "Take that, you dragon!" he yelled, pointing his sword at me.

Suddenly I felt very happy to be home. My mother put milk and cookies on the table for Charlie and me. They were the best. Then my grandmother Nooma joined us in the kitchen. She and my grandfather live in an apartment that's attached to our house. One summer when I was six, my father turned our spare room into an apartment for them. She and my grandfather have lived with us ever since.

After I had a few cookies, Mom made me describe every detail of the makeover. Mom asked me a thousand questions. I could tell that Nooma was very proud. Even Charlie seemed happy. When Mom explained that I was going to have my picture taken, Charlie grinned, dropped his sword on the floor, and climbed into my lap.

It was funny, but my nervous feeling went away. As a matter of fact, I felt better than I had all day. And I realized that I was actually looking forward to tomorrow.

# Chapter Seven

*Sabrina calls Allison. Charlie answers.*

SABRINA: Hello. Is Allison there, please?

CHARLIE: I'm Spiderman!

SABRINA: Hi, Spiderman. Listen, this is Wonder Woman. Could you please put Allison on the phone?

CHARLIE: Okay.

ALLISON: Hello?

SABRINA: Hi, Allison, it's Sabs. Listen, do you know which pages we're supposed to read for social studies? I know I wrote them down, but now I can't seem to find them anywhere.

ALLISON: Sure. We're supposed to read all of Chapter Seven and then answer the questions at the end.

SABRINA: Did you do it yet?

ALLISON: Yeah. It's easy.

SABRINA: So what are you up to?

| | |
|---|---|
| ALLISON: | Not much. Reading. |
| SABRINA: | Okay, well, I guess I'd better get to work on this. Thanks. |
| ALLISON: | Sure, Sabs. See you tomorrow. |
| SABRINA: | Okay, bye. |
| ALLISON: | Oh, by the way, Sabrina? |
| SABRINA: | Yeah? |
| ALLISON: | *Belle* called. |
| SABRINA: | Are you kidding me?! Allison! What did they say? |
| ALLISON: | They want to use me in a shoot tomorrow after school in Widmere. |
| SABRINA: | That's incredible! See, Allison, I knew they'd call you, no matter what Stacy said. Wow! I bet you'll become a famous model now. I knew it. |
| ALLISON: | I doubt that. Anyway, you'd better get to work if you want to get that assignment done tonight. |
| SABRINA: | I guess you're right. But this is so exciting! Well, I guess I'll talk to you some more about it in school tomorrow. Bye, Al. |
| ALLISON: | Bye, Sabs. |

*Sabrina calls Randy.*

SABRINA: Hi, Randy. It's Sabrina.

RANDY: Hi, Sabs. What's up?

SABRINA: Listen, I can't stay on the phone too long, I haven't done my social studies yet. But I just had to call. I have the most incredible news.

RANDY: What is it?

SABRINA: Guess. What is the great news we've all been waiting to hear? Think about it.

RANDY: School's closed for the rest of the year.

SABRINA: No, silly. *Belle* called Allison. They want her to model for them after school tomorrow.

RANDY: Wow, that's totally awesome! I'm so proud of Al.

SABRINA: Me, too. Isn't it great? I'm so excited. Anyway, I really have to go. I have to get started on this social studies right away.

RANDY: Okay. See you tomorrow, Sabs.

SABRINA: Okay. Bye, Randy.

EMILY: Hello?

**Sabrina calls Katie.**

SABRINA: Hi, Emily. It's Sabrina. Can I talk to Katie, please?

EMILY: Just a minute. Katie! Sabrina's on the phone for you, but don't stay on too long — I'm expecting a call.

KATIE: Hi, Sabs.

SABRINA: Hi, Katie. I really shouldn't be calling you at all. I haven't even started my social studies yet. But I just couldn't wait.

KATIE: What is it? Is everything all right?

SABRINA: Even better than all right — incredible! *Belle* called Allison and she's modeling for them tomorrow afternoon.

KATIE: That's wonderful! Al must be so excited!

SABRINA: I know. Isn't it great? I don't know how I'm going to concentrate on my homework now. Anyway, I have to hang up now.

KATIE: Same here. My sister needs to use the phone.

SABRINA: Okay. See you tomorrow. Bye.

KATIE: Bye.

## Chapter Eight

When I woke up the next morning, my nervous feeling had returned. The thought of school made my stomach jumpy. I was pretty sure that everyone would want to talk about the shoot and I was right.

"Allison!" shouted Katie, Randy, and Sabrina when I walked into school. "We've been waiting for you! Aren't you excited? What time does the shoot start? Did they tell you what you'll be wearing? I'll bet you'll have to wear a lot of makeup." The questions were coming so fast I couldn't answer any of them. But that didn't seem to matter. They kept chattering away until I had put my coat and books into my locker.

Randy looked at me and asked, "Hey, Al, is anything wrong? You don't look excited at all."

Now they were all staring at me, and I felt even jumpier than before. I tried to think of a way, without hurting their feelings, to tell them that I didn't want to talk about modeling or *Belle*, but I couldn't think of anything to say. The warning bell rang, so I just mumbled, "No, I'm fine, I'll see you later." I almost knocked people over in the hallway, trying to get away from all the questions. Besides, what could I say? I hadn't gone on the shoot yet.

At lunchtime I decided to go to the library instead of the cafeteria. The thought of food made me sick, so I picked out a book and sat down in a corner. I knew that Katie, Randy, and Sabrina would wonder what was wrong with me, but I just didn't feel like talking. I knew they meant well, but when I get nervous it's best for me to be alone and work things out for myself.

The day went by fast and before I knew it, it was three o'clock. I packed up my books and walked toward the exit where my mother said she'd be waiting for me. When I got to the car, Stacy was already sitting in the backseat. She must have been excited about the shoot, even if it did mean riding in a car with me to get there. I had to admit, I was a little excited myself.

To my surprise, Stacy smiled at me when she saw me. "Hi, Allison!" she sang out cheerfully.

I wasn't sure how to react. I couldn't imagine

that Stacy was happy to see me. I climbed into the front next to my mother. I still didn't really feel like talking, but I didn't have to worry. Stacy talked to my mom during the entire trip to Widmere. We found the football field pretty easily and my mother stopped the car at the gates in front of the field.

"Bye, Mom," I said, giving her a quick kiss and getting out of the car.

"Okay, sweetie, good-bye and good luck. Have fun," my mother said. "I guess I'll see you later. Stacy, does your mother know where to pick you girls up?"

"Oh, yes, Mrs. Cloud. I told her I'd call when I knew what time we'd be finished."

"Okay, then, bye-bye!" called my mother, pulling out of the parking lot.

I looked at Stacy, who was still smiling stiffly. She looked pretty nervous, and I felt the same way, so I tried to smile back. After all, we were going to spend the afternoon together so we had better learn to get along.

"Well, I guess we go over there," I said, noticing two trailers on the other side of the football field.

"Allison, I hope you didn't think I was rude

yesterday," Stacy said as we were walking along.

I looked at her in surprise.

"Oh, come on," she said, flipping her hair over her shoulder. "You didn't take me seriously, did you? Don't you always kid around with your friends like that?"

I never did, but I was surprised to hear her use the word "friend." I guess it showed on my face, because she went on quickly. "Well, we are sort of friends," said Stacy, "if you think about it. I mean, we don't know anyone here except each other, and since we are from the same school, and in the same class, I figure we might as well stick together. You know, kind of help each other out?"

I didn't know what to say. Stacy had said some pretty rotten things in the past, but here she was practically apologizing. I began to wonder if I had misjudged her.

"Yeah, sure, I guess so," I mumbled.

Stacy sighed with relief. It was almost as if *she* was the one who was afraid of how *I* was going to treat *her* at the shoot.

When we got to the other side of the field, Darla Jones directed us toward one of the trailers, where she said Maryann would give us the clothes we were going to wear.

"Is this where we're going to have our pictures taken?" I asked. It seemed sort of strange to me that they had asked us to come to a football field.

"Yes," said Darla. "We're going to do an 'afternoon at the game' type of thing. It'll be terrific. You'll see."

Inside the trailer, Kelly Kay, the girl I had met on Saturday, waved from a corner. Maryann was buttoning her into a long, green dress. "Hi, Allison!" Kelly called out.

Stacy looked at me in surprise. I could tell she was wondering how I had managed to have a friend there already.

"Hi, girls. Come on in," said Maryann. "We have to get moving. We're on a really tight schedule, and we don't have much daylight left." She finished buttoning Kelly's dress and gave her a little pat on the back. "Okay, Kelly, you're done. David and Candy will do your hair and makeup in the other trailer."

At the mention of David's name, my scalp began to tingle. I wondered what he was going to do to my hair this time.

Maryann was rummaging through a pile of clothes. "Let's see. Why don't you try these on?" she said.

I changed quickly. There was a gathered denim miniskirt, a pink T-shirt, ribbed pink tights, and to top it all off, one of those suede jackets with all the fringe, and a pair of matching brown suede boots. I felt pretty silly in all that flashy stuff, but I tried to act as normal as possible.

Stacy was changing into a big, bulky, gray turtleneck sweater and a pair of black stretch pants. She wore a pair of short, black boots with straps around the ankles.

After we were dressed, Maryann looked us over, nodded to herself, and told us to hurry over to the other trailer.

"Allison," Stacy said with a sigh as we walked along, "your outfit is so nice."

"Really?" I answered doubtfully. "I feel silly in it."

"Oh, no," she assured me. "You look really great. I wish I'd gotten to wear something like that. I really hate gray," she went on. "It's such a bad color on me. I wanted to say something to Maryann, but I was scared."

"Scared?" It was hard to imagine Stacy being scared of anything.

"Yeah," she said. "I'm so nervous about this whole thing. I've never done anything like this before, and we don't know anyone here. I keep hoping I won't do something wrong."

"No one here is a professional model," I pointed out. "I bet if we pay attention and do what they tell us, we'll do fine."

She reached out to squeeze my arm. "Thanks, Allison," she said, smiling. "You know what? I'm really glad you're here."

I smiled back. I was really starting to have second thoughts about Stacy.

On our way, we caught up with the tall Black girl we'd met at the makeover. She was wearing a stretchy black miniskirt, bright yellow turtleneck, matching yellow tights, and a long, red cardigan sweater. On her feet were black suede loafers with yellow and black polka-dot bows.

"Hi," she said. "I'm Keisha Lewis."

Stacy and I introduced ourselves. Keisha told us that she lived in Widmere and that her older brother went to Green Acres High School. "He's on the football team here," she explained. "But I guess you'll meet him later. He's changing with the guys in the locker room. See you down on the field."

I turned to Stacy and asked, "What did she mean when she said her brother's changing with the guys and we would meet him later?"

"I don't know," she replied, looking as confused as I felt.

We climbed the steps to the trailer. Inside, Kelly was sitting in a chair, and David was wrapping a flowered scarf around her long, red hair like a headband.

"There you go, honey. That looks perfect," he told her. "Now head on over to Candy so she can do your face.

"Well, hello!" he said. "I've been waiting for you two. Allison, bring that gorgeous head of hair over here."

I walked over and sat down on the chair in front of him. *Here goes*, I thought.

The first thing he did was to pull out my ponytail holder, which didn't surprise me at all.

"We're going to keep your hair loose today, honey," he told me. "We're just going to fluff it out a little, add a little body, a little pizzazz."

I had no idea what he was talking about, and I certainly didn't know what he meant by pizzazz, but I didn't want to be difficult, so I nodded.

He brushed through my hair for a few moments, and then he handed me the brush. "Now, Allison," he said, "I want you to bend over from the waist and flip your hair upside-down. Then you can brush the underside of your hair. That will give you a fuller look."

I bent over and started brushing. When I was finished, I flipped my hair back and into place. I could tell it was really sticking out, and I was sure it looked ridiculous.

Then David parted my hair on the side, much farther over than I do it. Finally, he spritzed it with all this spray.

Candy had finished with Kelly, so I walked over and sat down so she could do my makeup. "Hi, Allison," said Candy. "Now just have a seat and relax. First I'm going to put a foundation on you to help even out your skin tone." She started to spread some liquid makeup on my face with a tiny sponge.

"It feels like you're putting on a lot," I told her.

She smiled. "Oh, you have to wear a lot more makeup in front of the camera than you would for a regular day," she explained.

I didn't tell her that on my regular days I didn't wear makeup, so any makeup at all was more than I usually wore.

After the foundation, she applied three colors of eyeshadow, eyeliner, eyebrow pencil, and mascara. It was really hard to keep from blinking while she was doing all that stuff to my eyes. Then came two shades of blush, lip pencil, and lipstick. When she was all finished, I felt as if my face was caked with mud. I wondered if I looked like a circus clown.

David had just finished combing Stacy's blond hair into a high ponytail, which he tied with a pink bow. It was her turn for makeup, and she begged me to wait for her. Since I wasn't sure I wanted anyone else to see me looking like this, and I wasn't in any rush to leave, I agreed.

"Okay, girls," Candy said. "You're both ready. Report to Darla out on the field." She laughed. "Why do I feel like I'm sending you out to play football when I say that?"

I tried to laugh, too. But as Stacy and I headed for the door, I realized that I was as nervous as I would have been if I were actually going to play a football game.

## Chapter Nine

The first thing I noticed as Stacy and I approached the bleachers was a group of lights set up on stands and reflecting off of big, white umbrellas. Then I noticed three girls sitting on a bench, Kelly, Keisha, and the Asian girl. Darla and Maryann fussed with their clothes and hair. The third, and most surprising, thing was five high school guys dressed in football uniforms.

"Do you see what I see?" Stacy asked me, her eyes wide open.

"I guess that's what Keisha meant when she said her brother and the other guys were getting dressed," I said.

Just then, a short man with dark, curly hair and a mustache came running up to us. There were two cameras hanging around his neck. "And finally I am to see my other two," he said, throwing his arms upward and breaking into a big smile. *"Ah, sì, che bellezza!"*

Darla Jones walked briskly over to where we were standing. "This is Lorenzo Fortuna," she told us. "He's our photographer. Lorenzo, here are Stacy Hansen and Allison Cloud."

Lorenzo took my hand and began to talk very quickly. "Ah, *Signorina! Come sta?* How do you do? What did you say is your name? Cloud? This is like that which floats in the sky? In Italian we say *nuvola. Signorina* Allison *La Nuvola!*" He smiled and bent over to kiss my hand.

I had no idea what to do. No one had ever kissed my hand before. "Uh, thank you. I mean, nice to meet you," I stammered.

Then Lorenzo Fortuna grabbed Stacy's hand. "*Buon giorno, Signorina.* I am very happy to meet you," he said. He bent over and suddenly kissed her hand.

Stacy looked over at me and we both tried not to laugh. "Now we must start right away! *Ora!* Now! We begin!" Lorenzo called out, clapping his hands. "First the *signorinas*. Ladies, please!"

He arranged the five of us. We sat on the bench. I was in between Keisha and the Asian girl.

"Hi," I whispered to her. "I'm Allison. Allison Cloud."

"I'm Suzi Kim," she told me.

The guys in the football uniforms were still standing over to one side, watching us.

I turned to Keisha. "Why are they here?" I asked her. "Your brother and those other guys."

"Oh, they're supposed to be in some photographs with us. You know, kind of make it seem more like we're at a *real* football game," she answered. "That's Chris, my brother, number 43." I looked toward where she was pointing. Chris saw us looking at him and waved, and Keisha waved back.

"The rest of the guys are pretty nice, too," Keisha continued. "That's Tyler, with the blond hair, number 12. Next to him is Freddy, number 73. Number 22 is Andy, and over there, with the curly, black hair, is Bruce the Moose."

I wanted to ask her how Bruce had gotten that nickname, but just then Lorenzo started yelling out directions. "And now, please to put the arms around each other! Yes, like friends!" he said, motioning wildly with his arms.

I put my left arm around Suzi and my right around Keisha.

"This guy's a little nutty, I think," Suzi said under her breath.

Keisha giggled. "That's for sure," she said.

Lorenzo pointed at Keisha excitedly. "This is right! This is good! *Splendida!* Like this one, *Signorina* Keisha, she looks to be having the good time. Please to smile, laugh like this, everybody!"

At first it was kind of hard to smile just because someone holding a camera told you to, and I felt kind of silly and embarrassed. The football players had stopped talking to each other and were watching us, and I felt really self-conscious. But Lorenzo was so crazy, and the way he ran around snapping his camera and yelling out directions in both English and Italian was so funny that before I knew it I was laughing along with everyone else.

Finally Lorenzo decided he was ready to take some pictures of us with the guys.

"Gentlemen, please! *Presto!* Now I am ready!" he called.

Keisha's brother and the four other guys drifted over to where we were sitting.

"*A sinistra!* To the left? *Si metta qui!* Stand here!" said Lorenzo, arranging them in a line behind us. And finally, "*Che bravi! Non si muova!* Don't move!"

He moved around us quickly, snapping pic-

69

tures from different angles. Suddenly he stopped and lowered his camera.

"Please!" he called out. *"Signorina La Nuvola.* The hair please! We must see more of this beautiful hair! *Signorina La Nuvola!"*

Suddenly I realized he was talking to me, but I had no idea what he wanted me to do.

"Yes?" I called out, looking up at him nervously.

"The hair, *Signorina,* please! Show me more! Please do not hide the hair."

Then I heard a voice behind me say, "I think he wants you to put some of that pretty hair in front of your shoulders where he can see it."

I turned my head and saw Bruce, the guy with the curly, black hair, standing behind me.

"Uh, thanks," I said, picking up a handful of my hair and tossing it in front of my shoulder. I could feel my face burning.

*"Ah, sì, brava!"* called Lorenzo happily, snapping away.

After some more pictures, Lorenzo told us that he wanted us to play a little football. "You know, how they do, like this?" he asked, putting his arms over Chris and Tyler's shoulders.

Lorenzo divided us into two groups. Keisha,

Suzi, and I were in one group with Andy and Bruce. He had us pretend that we were planning our strategy for the game, then clap and break, just like a real football team. Then he had us line up on the field in a formation.

Over and over again, he had us pretend to start a game of touch football. We had a lot of fun passing the ball around, pretending to block each other really hard, running from one end of the field to the other. After a while, we were all pretty breathless, and Lorenzo told us to take a little break.

David and Candy came over to each of us to check our hair and makeup; then some of the other people started handing out juice and granola bars. I sat down on the bleachers to finish my snack. Bruce came over and sat next to me.

"That was some workout," he said, smiling. "You know, when I first heard about this modeling stuff, I thought it was something only a real airhead would do, but it's not turning out to be as easy as it looks," he said.

"That's what I thought, too," I told him. "My friends had to talk me into it."

"Really? Same here," he said, grinning. "Hey, what's your name?"

"Allison Cloud."

"I'm Bruce. Bruce Cornell."

He smiled at me, and I couldn't help noticing that his eyes were a very unusual shade of green.

Just then Lorenzo called us all over to the end zone. This time he put all the guys on one team and he lined us girls up along the sideline. "You cheer, yes? You yell and smile for nice boys!" he told us. Then he told the guys to pretend that they were scoring a touchdown against their biggest rival.

They did a really good job of making the touchdown look like a struggle, considering the fact that there was no other team. They ran into the end zone as if there was a steamroller after them, then gave each other high fives, just like a real game. We all yelled and clapped until our hands hurt. Lorenzo made the boys do the scene over a few more times before he was satisfied. He seemed really happy with us girls, except when Stacy started doing splits in the air and cartwheels, like a cheerleader. "You calm down, yes, *Signorina* Hansen? Gymnastics this is not."

After a while, Lorenzo gave us another break. "Now we must the lights move, the cameras reload. *Sì!* This goes well."

Bruce ran off the field toward me and took his helmet off. "Whew! This is almost as tough as a real game! Hey, I don't remember seeing you at any of the games. Are you from Widmere?" he asked.

"Acorn Falls," I told him.

"Oh," he said, looking a little disappointed.

"Why do they call you Moose?" I asked him.

His face got red. "Oh, that," he said. "Well, it's because I'm so big. I guess sometimes I get a little rough on the field. One day someone started calling me Moose, and the name stuck."

Just then, Lorenzo walked over to us. "*Sì, sì,* this I like! These two are very friendly, one can see this in the eyes. *Signorina La Nuvola* and Mr. Green Eyes. Please, I want to have just the two of you together now. *Capisce?* You understand?"

I was sort of embarrassed by this, but I was glad I would be posing with Bruce. I liked talking to him.

It was actually Bruce who came up with the funny idea for the pictures. He told Lorenzo that American football players are always trying to dump water buckets on each other's heads. Lorenzo really liked the idea. No one thought we should use real water, so we filled up a bucket

73

with some leaves.

Then Bruce sat on a bench and I pretended to sneak up behind him with the bucket of leaves and dump it on his head. Lorenzo took picture after picture.

After the solo shots, Lorenzo took a few more pictures of us all together until it got dark.

Then Darla thanked us and announced that she would need all the girls for another shoot on Thursday at the Widmere Mall. She promised to call our parents and tell them the details.

Stacy and I walked over to the pay phone near the locker rooms to call her mother. While Stacy was on the phone, Bruce walked by. He stopped and wiped his forehead.

"Boy," he said, "this took such a long time, I don't know how I'm going to finish all my homework tonight."

"Me, either," I said, shaking my head.

He waited. "Well," he began, "it sure was fun working with you."

I swallowed. Suddenly I couldn't think of anything to say to him. "Yeah, same here," I finally answered.

"Well, maybe we'll see each other again sometime," he said.

"Come on, Allison, we have to go change," Stacy said after hanging up the phone. "My mother's on her way to pick us up."

"Well, bye, Bruce," I said.

"Bye, Allison," he answered, and walked off toward the locker room.

"He's cute," Stacy said, turning to me.

"Yeah," I answered, "I guess he is."

## Chapter Ten

I wasn't exactly sure why, but I decided to wear my hair loose the next day instead of fixing it into my usual braid. I even decided that I would brush it upside-down every day the way David had shown me. It looked sort of wild and fluffy.

I had planned on wearing my usual jeans and sweater, but somehow it didn't feel quite right with my hair. So I put on an oversized, yellow T-shirt that Sabrina had talked me into buying. Then I put on a pair of stonewashed overalls with yellow-and-white-striped cuffs and pockets, yellow socks, and a plain white pair of tennis shoes. At first, I felt kind of like a sunflower, but it was too late to change.

I'm sure my mother was surprised when I walked into the kitchen. I hadn't worn my hair loose since I was about five and she had never seen me wear that T-shirt, but she just smiled and asked me what I wanted for breakfast. I was glad. I didn't feel like explaining myself. At the last minute, I decided to pull on a hat to keep my hair from blowing around outside.

When I got to school, Sabs, Katie, and Randy were waiting by my locker.

"Allison! You're finally here! Why didn't you call last night? We all left messages," Sabs exclaimed.

"Yes, Allison, we're dying to know what happened!" Katie added.

I opened my locker and smiled at them guiltily. "I'm really sorry, guys, but I got home so late, and I hadn't done any of my homework," I explained.

"Figures," said Randy jokingly. "Allison was busy doing homework — as usual."

"Forget that!" said Sabs, starting to hop up and down with excitement. "Tell us what happened!"

"What was it like?" asked Katie.

"Are you a famous model yet?" asked Randy, putting one hand behind her head and the other on her hip and striking a pose.

"Well —" I began. I wasn't sure where to start. It seemed as if so much had happened since I had

seen them last, even though it had only been yesterday. "First we were in these trailers —"

"Trailers?" asked Sabrina, surprised.

"Why, were they going to take you camping?"
asked Randy.

"Sshh!" said Katie. "Let her tell us!"

"Well," I said, "they had two trailers, one for
clothes and one for makeup and hair."

"Oh, my gosh," said Katie, "it sounds so exciting."

I took off my jacket and hat and started to put
them in my locker.

Sabrina's eyes popped. "Allison!" she yelped.
"Your hair!"

"I never thought I'd see the day," Randy said,
staring at my outfit.

It took me a second to figure out what they
were talking about. I had forgotten about my hair
because of the hat.

"You look incredible," Katie told me.

"Thanks," I said, a little embarrassed.

"See, Allison," Sabs went on, "I told you that
T-shirt was right for you. And your hair! It looks
so nice. You should wear it that way all the time. "

I didn't know what to say. I had to admit it
seemed silly that I usually wore my hair in a

braid. Suddenly the warning bell rang. Everyone ran to their lockers and gathered their books and papers. Sabrina and I had math together so we ran up the stairs.

Ms. Munson, the math teacher, is really old and really strict. I was worried that we would be late, but Sabs and I rushed through the door just as the final bell rang.

I was trying to concentrate on what Ms. Munson was writing on the board when Jerry Walker, who was sitting behind me, tapped me on the shoulder and passed me a note.

I reached for the note slowly and carefully, terrified that Ms. Munson would notice. She's got a reputation for catching people who pass notes and making them read the notes out loud. I carefully unfolded the note, wondering who had been brave enough to send it. The note said, "Come to Fitzie's today after school — I have a SURPRISE!"

The note wasn't signed and I didn't recognize the handwriting. I slowly lifted my eyes from the paper and looked around the room. Sabs was drawing little moons and stars all over the paper in front of her. She obviously hadn't sent it.

Just then, Stacy, who was sitting in the front row, dropped her pencil on the floor. As she bent over to pick it up, she turned her head toward me and smiled.

I smiled back, but just a little, so Ms. Munson wouldn't notice. I was really beginning to change my mind about Stacy. I mean, she had been so friendly yesterday at the shoot. Besides, it was fun to have someone else in school who knew all about crazy Lorenzo Fortuna and David the hairstylist and Maryann and Candy and Darla Jones.

For the rest of the day, I wondered about Stacy's surprise. I decided it wouldn't hurt to pass by Fitzie's on my way home from school and find out. What I hadn't counted on was Randy, Sabs, and Katie going to Fitzie's, too. "We all decided it would be a perfect time for you to tell us all about yesterday," Sabs explained.

"Yeah," said Katie, smiling, "none of us have to be home right away and we'll have plenty of time."

"It's a celebration for you," Sabs explained.

It didn't seem like a good idea to go to Fitzie's with them and meet Stacy there at the same time, but I didn't really see how I could get out of it. I couldn't make up some excuse or say I didn't feel like it if I was actually planning on going. I guess

I could have just gone home, but I felt kind of bad. Even though I had managed to tell Sabs, Katie, and Randy something about the shoot during lunch, I knew they were still dying to hear every detail.

Finally, I decided that there was nothing wrong with going to Fitzie's with them and then saying "hi" to Stacy while I was there and finding out what her big surprise was. Besides, maybe it would be a chance for my friends to see that Stacy wasn't as bad as they thought.

When we arrived at Fitzie's, it looked like I had nothing to worry about, because I didn't see Stacy anywhere. I did see Eva, B.Z., and Laurel sitting in a booth near the front. I noticed that B.Z. looked different. She didn't seem to be wearing much makeup at all, which was unusual for her. But she looked really good. I wondered what they covered in her makeup workshop at the makeover.

"Well, I know what I'm having," Sabrina announced. "I've been dreaming of a brownie sundae all day."

"Sounds good," said Katie. "Maybe I'll have that, too."

"It's definitely chocolate-banana shake time

for me!" said Randy.

"What are you having, Allison?" Katie asked me.

All this looking around and feeling sneaky was giving me an upset stomach. "Um, I'm not really that hungry," I answered.

"Allison, you have to have something!" Sabs exclaimed in surprise. "This is your celebration, after all."

I could see I was going to have to have something if I didn't want to let them down. "Well, maybe I'll just get a cone or something," I said.

"A cone!" Randy exclaimed. "Al! This is a special occasion! You should have something totally amazing — like a banana boat!"

"It's Allison's celebration," Katie said, coming to my rescue. "She should order whatever she feels like having."

"So, what was everyone else like?" Sabs wanted to know. "You know, the other models. Were they really stuck-up?"

"Oh, no," I said quickly. "Everyone was really nice. I mean, it was fun. We all got along really well."

"You mean everyone but one person was nice," Randy said pointedly.

"I can only imagine what Stacy must have been like," Sabrina added.

"Did you have to be with her in a lot of the pictures?" Katie asked, looking at me sympathetically. "Was she really obnoxious?"

I knew it was time to try to explain about Stacy. "No," I said. "Stacy was okay. I mean, she was pretty nervous, but we all were."

"Oh, come on, Allison," said Sabs. "You're always too nice about everything. You can tell *us* the truth. How bad was she?"

"No, really," I answered. "She was very nice. She said she was glad I was there."

They all stared at me in disbelief.

"You must be kidding!"

"Allison, after all the things she's said and done to all of us, you didn't believe her, did you?" Randy demanded.

"Well," I began, trying to figure out how to explain what I meant. "I sort of got to thinking, and I decided that maybe Stacy just acts that way in school because she's nervous that people won't like her."

"Well," said Sabrina, "if that's what she's worried about, she should try being nice to people for a change." Katie and Randy just nodded their heads in agreement.

Our food came, and out of the corner of my eye I saw Stacy walk through the door. She was carrying one of those big manila envelopes under her arm, and she looked really excited. She sat down in a booth with Eva, B.Z., and Laurel.

No one at my table had noticed Stacy yet. I decided to change the subject. It didn't seem as if I could make Sabs, Randy, and Katie understand that Stacy wasn't so bad.

"So," I said brightly, trying to keep one eye on Stacy as I spoke, "I guess I haven't told you guys about the photographer yet."

They looked at me with interest.

"Well," I went on, "he was really unbelievable. His name is Lorenzo Fortuna —"

Katie giggled. "What kind of a name is that?" she asked.

"I'm pretty sure it's Italian," I told her. "Half the time he spoke to us in Italian, and we had no idea what he was talking about."

I glanced quickly at Stacy's table. She had pulled something out of the manila envelope and everyone at her table crowded around her, looking at it.

"Tell us more about the guys," Sabs said.

"Well, some of them were really nice," I said, thinking of Bruce.

"They were from the high school team, right?" Katie asked.

"Was it really embarrassing to have to model with them?" asked Sabs.

"Did you have to do a lot of corny stuff?" asked Randy.

"Well, kind of," I began. "We were supposed to pretend to be at a football game —"

Just then I was interrupted by the sound of Stacy shrieking my name. "ALLISON!!"

I looked up and saw her hurrying toward our table. Sabs rolled her eyes, Randy made a face, and Katie sighed.

"There you are!" Stacy squealed. "I didn't think you were here yet!"

"Um, hi, Stacy," I said quietly.

Stacy didn't seem to notice the cold reaction she was getting from my table. She grabbed me by the arm and pulled me up from my chair.

"You're never going to believe this!" she said. "It's the surprise I told you about. I have the pictures!"

"Th-the p-pictures?" I stammered. "The ones from the shoot?" How could Stacy have those pictures already?

"Oh wow!" exclaimed Sabrina, forgetting that she was talking to Stacy.

"Yes, silly!" said Stacy directly to me, completely ignoring Sabrina. "The pictures from yesterday. Today while we were in school I had my mother call Lorenzo Fortuna. He had just finished developing them." She started to pull me toward her table.

"These aren't really the actual pictures they're going to use," Stacy explained as we slid into her booth. "These are only the contact sheets. The pictures are hard to see because each frame is so small. Anyway, *Belle* chooses which shots they're going to use from these sheets."

"This is so cool!" Sabrina gushed, coming up to the table. I could tell she was really excited. Stacy just ignored her and pressed me further into the booth.

My eyes traveled to the pictures. They were kind of hard to see, but there we were. There was the picture of all of us with our arms linked, and of the guys making a touchdown, and the pictures of Bruce and me and the water bucket. It was so strange to see them, but I have to say, standing there with all those people around, I started to feel sort of proud.

"Allison," said Eva as she huddled over the pictures, "your hair looks so good like this. Why don't you wear it down more often? And I love your clothes!"

"These are great shots," commented Laurel.

"You look terrific, Allison!" B.Z. gushed. "Especially with that gorgeous guy."

"What gorgeous guy?" asked Sabrina, jumping up and down and trying to get a peek at the pictures.

Suddenly Laurel looked up and stared at Sabrina. "What are you doing at *our* table?" she asked loudly.

"I came over to see Allison's pictures," Sabs answered just as loudly.

"Allison's pictures?" Eva asked, and started to laugh. "Mrs. Hansen got these pictures for Stacy."

"Nobody asked you to join us," Laurel added in a really snotty tone of voice.

"Some people are naturally rude," huffed Eva.

I put the contact sheet I was holding down on the table. I started to tell them that Sabs was my friend and welcome any place I was welcome. But before I could get a word out Stacy cut in. "Well, Sabrina, I'm only supposed to show these pictures to Allison since she was at the shoot. You'll just have to see the final version when it comes out in the magazine."

Sabrina looked at me for a moment and then whirled around and ran toward the table where Katie and Randy were sitting.

"Excuse me, Stacy," I said. "Thank you for showing me the pictures but I have to go now." I knew I should have said something about the way they had just treated Sabs, but at that moment I just wanted to get away from them.

"Oh, but you haven't seen these sheets yet," Stacy said as if she hadn't heard me.

I cleared my throat and tried again. "Stacy, thanks for letting me see the pictures, but I've got to go now."

"This is a particularly good shot, don't you think?" said Stacy as she held the photographs right in front of my face.

"Stacy, will you please let me out of this booth!" I demanded.

"What?" said Stacy, looking surprised. "Oh, I'm sorry, Allison, I didn't know you wanted to leave." She stood up and let me out of the booth. Then she said, "Allison, I'm glad you came over to look at the pictures, really," and she smiled.

By the time I got back to our table, Randy was the only one left.

"Where did Sabrina and Katie go?" I asked.

"I don't know," said Randy, "but Sabrina sure was upset when she came back here. She ran out of here real fast and Katie ran after her. What happened?"

"Well, we were all trying to look at the pictures and Eva and Laurel asked Sabrina why she was at their table. She said she came to look at my pictures and Eva said they weren't my pictures, they were Stacy's pictures, and that she was being really rude."

"They did what?" screamed Randy. "I hope you told them they were all a bunch of bingoheads!"

"Well, I didn't exactly get a chance, they —"

"Allison, I can't believe you'd stand by and let those jerks pick on Sabrina. No wonder she ran out of here so fast."

I looked down at the table. Randy was right, I should have stuck up more for Sabrina.

"I'm going to Sabrina's house right now," Randy said, standing up.

"Yes, I'll come with you." I stood up and started to put on my coat.

Just then Stacy came running up to our table.

"Allison!" she called. "I'm so glad you haven't left yet. I almost forgot. I have something really important to talk to you about. "

Randy glared at Stacy and then at me. "I'm leaving *now*, Allison," and she turned and ran toward the door.

"Randy! Wait!" I called out to her but she was gone in a flash.

"Allison," Stacy said, tapping her foot impatiently, "are you listening to me? I need a ride to the shoot on Thursday."

Stacy started explaining why her mother couldn't give her a ride, but I wasn't listening. If only *Belle* had picked someone else to be a model and not me! Suddenly my life seemed like a total mess.

## Chapter Eleven

That night, for the first time since I could remember, Sabrina didn't call me. In fact, nobody else called me, either. Except for Stacy, that is. She called to make sure that she could get a ride with me to Widmere the next day. I tried calling Sabrina but the line was busy all evening. I decided to get to school super early and straighten everything out in the morning.

When I got to school the next day no one was waiting for me by my locker. It was kind of strange since we usually meet at the lockers before school. I always wait for Sabrina and we walk to math class together.

When I got to class, I was surprised to see that Sabrina was already there. I sat down in my usual spot next to her.

"Hi," I said. "How come you didn't wait for me?"

"Sorry. I guess I forgot," she said, and began

rummaging through her bag for something. As soon as she found what she was looking for, she buried her head in her notebook.

I knew that Sabs was really mad at me but I didn't know how to explain what had happened. I sat down at my desk to think of a way to apologize for not sticking up for her. The harder I thought about it, the worse I felt and I ended up not saying anything to her.

Later that morning during English class, Sabs, Randy, and Katie ignored me, and I felt worse than ever.

"Today we're going to have an in-class assignment," Ms. Staats began.

A moan went up from the class.

Everyone started taking out pieces of paper and opening their English books, so I did the same. The assignment was pretty easy. It was a long list of sentences and we were supposed to identify the parts of speech for each one. Before I knew it, I found myself daydreaming about what the shoot might be like that afternoon. I wondered what they wanted us to do this time and what we might be wearing.

Secretly I wished we were going back to the football field, so I could get a chance to see Bruce.

The more I thought about it, the more I decided Bruce was definitely very nice. Suddenly I looked up and Ms. Staats was collecting papers. Class was over and I hadn't finished the assignment!

"Now, before I let you go," said Ms. Staats, "I want to remind everyone that tomorrow is the deadline for *The Beacon*."

I gasped. I had completely forgotten about *The Beacon* and now I only had one day to write something. When Ms. Staats saw that I hadn't done the assignment she insisted that I get it to her by the end of the day. She said that it was going to help me with my submission for *The Beacon*. Trouble was, the only time I had free was lunch period because I had that shoot right after school.

Out of the corner of my eye, I saw Randy, Katie, and Sabrina hurry out of the room. Great! Now I wouldn't have a chance to talk to them during lunch as I had planned. I excused myself from Ms. Staats and went to the library to finish the assignment. I felt like kicking myself. I was beginning to think that modeling for *Belle* was the worst thing that had ever happened to me. Nothing had gone right since I went to the makeover on Saturday.

I finished the work and ran downstairs to put it in Ms. Staats's mailbox in the school office. I flew in and out so fast, that I didn't give the weird secretary, the one everyone calls the Pencil, a chance to ask questions. By the time I got back to the cafeteria I didn't see Katie, Randy, or Sabrina, anywhere. I did see Stacy and her group sitting at one of the tables. They were absolutely the last people I needed to see right then. I turned around and ran out of the cafeteria. I went back to the library and looked for the saddest book I could find. Then I sat in a corner reading for the rest of the lunch period.

# Chapter Twelve

After school my mother dropped us off at the entrance to the Widmere Mall. Stacy and I walked to Giggles, a clothing store that had been closed for the shoot.

This time I had to wear a big brown turtleneck sweater and plaid wool skirt. The sweater was really heavy and kind of itchy. Stacy got a pair of pink corduroy pants with matching suspenders, and a pink-and-lavender-striped long-sleeved T-shirt. She changed immediately and began posing.

"Well, Allison," Stacy said to me, "this time I guess *I* got the nicer outfit," which may have been true, but it didn't seem like a very nice thing to say.

Maryann sent us on to David and Candy, who had set up their things on a counter in a corner of the store.

This time Stacy went first. David explained

that we were supposed to have different hairstyles from last time, and he began rolling Stacy's hair up into hot rollers.

"Now we just wait ten minutes, and then we can take them out," he told Stacy.

Then it was my turn. I walked over and sat on a stool in front of him. I was hoping he would make an exception to the different hairstyles rule and let me wear my hair down again, but he began brushing it straight up. Then he fastened it into a very high ponytail on top of my head. Finally he divided the hair of the ponytail into tiny strands and braided it into lots of little braids. I couldn't help thinking that it probably looked a little silly.

When David was finished with me, he called Stacy over. He began taking out her rollers. As he unrolled them one by one, Stacy's hair fell in soft, blond curls down her back.

"Beautiful!" David announced. "We're not going to do another thing to it."

While Lorenzo was fiddling with the lights, Darla explained the idea of the shoot to us.

"This time we want to make it seem like you're all a bunch of friends shopping for school clothes together," she said. "And of course you'll be shopping for *Belle* fashions," she added with a smile.

This time Kelly was wearing a white top with a ruffled collar and a pair of gray wool shorts with tights underneath. Suzi had on a red turtle-neck and a black-and-white-checkered miniskirt. Keisha was wearing a turquoise sweater-dress. I couldn't help noticing that I liked what everyone else was wearing a lot more than what I had on.

"Now for the 'school flavor,'" said Darla. She picked up a canvas bag, opened it, and began looking through it. "Kelly, why don't you hold this?" she said, handing Kelly a speckled note-book.

"And let's give Suzi these." She pulled out a small stack of books held together by a strap — the kind that kids from olden days used.

"Allison, please put these on."

I couldn't believe what I saw — a pair of tor-toiseshell eyeglasses! It didn't seem fair. I didn't have to wear glasses in real life, so I didn't see why I had to wear them for a stupid magazine! For some reason, Stacy went on and on about the glasses and how good I looked in them. At one point, I felt like telling her to shut up and let us get on with the shoot.

*"Si metta qui!* Stand here! *Capisce?* You understand?... *A sinistra!* To the left! ... *Piu presto!*
Faster!... That's it! Now, *non si muova!* Don't move
one inch ..."

Somehow, this time Lorenzo didn't seem quite
as entertaining. I wished he would talk to us only
in English.

One thing I noticed right away was how
incredibly hot the lights were. They seemed so
much hotter now than when we were outside on
the football field, where the air was fresh. My
heavy sweater was really starting to itch.

Stacy was having a great time, though. You
might even say she was really starting to ham it
up in front of the camera. She managed to get into
practically every picture.

As for me, I was getting hot and tired. At one
point, since we were supposed to look as if we
were shopping for clothes, I had to hold up a
dress on a hanger and show it to Suzi. Lorenzo
kept making us do the shot over. He must have
taken a million pictures of us in that pose. My
arm really started aching from trying to hold the
dress up for so long.

"Up, up!" Lorenzo yelled at me. "You are letting the arm to droop down!"

Lorenzo threw up his arms. *"Che seccatura! Impossible!"* He turned to me. *"Signorina,* you must not to frown when you are looking at this dress. You are supposed to be happy. *Lieta!* Happy! You understand? *Capisce?"*

I tried to smile, but one thing was for sure, happy was the furthest thing from the way I was feeling.

Finally, Darla announced a ten-minute break. I was exhausted. I pulled off those fake eyeglasses and stumbled toward a stool near the front of the store. The loafers that Maryann had given me to wear were about a size too small, and my aching feet were longing for a rest. I kicked off my shoes and leaned my head back against the store window.

Suddenly I heard a tapping on the glass behind my head. It was Bruce! I hopped up from my stool, still in my stocking feet, and hurried over to open the door for him.

"What are you doing here?" I asked him.

"I just stopped by to say 'hi,'" he said. "And to see how it was going. You looked great in there."

I felt my face burning. I wondered how long Bruce had been there. "Well, I certainly haven't felt great, that's for sure," I told him.

"Really? What's the matter — no fun model-ing without me?" he teased.

I smiled. What Bruce had said was closer to the truth than I wanted to admit. "The lights are so hot, and these clothes are really uncomfortable. And you know Lorenzo —"

Suddenly the door opened and Stacy walked out.

"Oh, hi!" she said to Bruce, smiling up at him.

"Stacy, this is Bruce Cornell. Bruce, this is Stacy Hansen. We're in the same class," I said.

"Nice to meet you," Stacy said, tossing her curls. "Listen, Allison, Darla sent me to get you. She wants to talk to you."

I looked at Bruce. "Okay, well, I'll see you."

He smiled. "Good luck with the rest of the shoot. Maybe I'll hang around a little while and watch or something."

I looked at Stacy, but she didn't seem to be heading back into the store. As I walked inside, I heard her say, "So, Bruce, what position do you play on the football team?"

"Allison," Darla said, "there's something I want to talk to you about. I think you have real potential in the modeling business." She put down the shirt she was folding. "Now don't get me wrong. Modeling is a difficult business, and for every girl who makes it there are a hundred others who get their hearts broken. But I'd like you to consider going to New York."

My heart skipped. *New York!* "Don't you think I'm too young?" I asked timidly.

"Not as far as modeling is concerned. You're tall and you look older than your real age."

My head was spinning. Darla Jones was actually suggesting that I go to New York and be a professional model!

"Don't say anything yet, Allison," Darla continued. "It's a big decision. Talk it over with your family. I'll give you a call on Monday."

I walked back onto the set in a daze. Lorenzo had me pose for some close-ups with Kelly. We tried on knitted scarves and gloves. I was so pre-occupied that Kelly kept having to nudge me with her elbow and whisper the directions to me.

Then Keisha, Stacy, and Suzi posed for some close-ups wearing jewelry. Finally, Lorenzo was finished with us. The shoot had lasted a lot longer than the one on Tuesday. It was six o'clock and I was exhausted.

While we were changing, Stacy turned to me and said in her sweetest voice, "Oh, Allison, will you call your mother to come pick you up?"

"Why?" I asked her. "I thought your mother was coming to get us."

"I called her and told her not to. She thinks I'm riding home with you." She giggled. "See, Bruce offered to drive me home, and my mother would be really mad if she found out."

I couldn't believe my ears. "You what?"

"I told you," she said, pulling a sweater over her head and tossing her curls back into place. "Bruce is driving me home, so I called my mother and told her not to come."

"Stacy, how could you do this to me?" I demanded. "You knew I was counting on getting a ride home with you!"

Stacy sighed loudly. "What's the big deal, Allison? Can't you just call your mother? Gosh, I don't know what's wrong with you. You've been in a really rotten mood all day."

I was close to tears. I couldn't believe that Bruce had offered Stacy a ride. And now, thanks to both of them, I was going to have to call home to get picked up. I should have known better than to count on Stacy. I never should have trusted her.

Grabbing my jacket, I stormed out of the dressing room. I was running so fast that I smacked straight into Bruce.

"Hey, hold on a minute," he said, catching me. "Where are you going? Didn't Stacy tell you?"

"Yes, she told me," I answered, clenching my fists and blinking back the tears.

"So, then, are you coming?" he asked.

"Coming where?"

"Back to Acorn Falls. I guess she didn't tell you. I wanted to offer you a ride home, but I just didn't get a chance to talk to you. Then Stacy told me you were supposed to go home with her, so I decided to offer her a ride, too."

"You wanted to give me a ride home?" I asked in disbelief.

Bruce smiled. "Yeah," he said, "but I knew it wouldn't be right not to offer one to Stacy, too, once I heard you were going home together."

I looked up at Bruce's green eyes and smiling face and was very tempted to take him up on his offer. But I knew very well that my parents wouldn't approve of my driving all that way at night with someone they hadn't even met.

"Thanks a lot, Bruce, but my parents are already on their way here," I fibbed. "You take Stacy home."

He looked disappointed. "You really can't

come?" he asked.

I felt a pang in my stomach. "I really can't," I said. "But thanks anyway."

"Well, someday when you're a famous model, I can say, 'Allison Cloud once refused a ride home from me.'"

"Who knows?" I said. "Darla offered to take me to New York and help me start a career there."

"Really?" Bruce said. "That's great. I mean, if that's what you want to do."

"Yeah, I'm not sure yet," I said. "Right now, all I want to do is go home and fall asleep!"

"Yeah, you must be really tired," he said. "Well, I guess I'm going to have to take Stacy home, since I already offered. I sure wish you were coming."

"So do I," I told him, and he smiled. I started to walk away. I knew I had to call home.

"Hey!" Bruce called out. "Maybe, if you decide not to go to New York, you can come to a game and watch me play sometime!"

"Sure, Moose!" I yelled back, and waved.

I found a phone nearby and called home. My mother answered. She was just putting dinner on the table, so it turned out that my father was the one who had to come pick me up.

While I sat there waiting for my father to arrive, I couldn't help wondering about Stacy and Bruce, driving all the way to Acorn Falls together. Stacy would be sitting there in the front seat, right next to him, smiling and talking and trying to make him laugh. Was he having fun? Did he wish I was there instead of Stacy? Did he even remember that I was the one who was supposed to be there? I couldn't believe that Stacy had done this to me. After all her talk about sticking together because we were the only Acorn Falls girls ... and I had actually started to think that we could be friends!

A real friend would never have lied to me like that, or stranded me somewhere without a ride home. I wished Sabs, Randy, and Katie were with me. I could really use someone to talk to.

About twenty minutes later, my father's car pulled up. I knew he must be pretty upset to have gotten there so quickly. I ran around to the passenger side and got in. My father pulled out of the parking lot without saying a word. I decided that now would be the wrong time to tell him what Darla Jones had said. Neither of us talked for several minutes.

Then my father cleared his throat. "Allison, I

haven't had much time to talk to you since this modeling assignment came up. I've had my doubts from the start, but your mother seems to think modeling would be good for you. I certainly hope your school work isn't affected by all the time you are spending having your picture taken. I'd like to think that you have greater ambitions than making a living from your good looks. You must never forget that you have a mind, too."

We drove the rest of the way in silence. I couldn't help thinking that the worst thing about this lecture was that he was probably right.

## Chapter Thirteen

When the alarm went off the next morning, I was so sleepy that I couldn't figure out what was making such a loud, ringing sound. I had a dream that Darla Jones had called to tell me I had to hurry up or I would miss my plane to New York.

I hadn't told my family about my having a chance to model in New York. I decided that I wanted to think it over for myself first.

I fumbled through the morning in a kind of haze. It was all I could do to stay awake. I pulled on a pair of white pants and the *Belle* sweatshirt, which was so long it almost reached my knees, left my hair hanging down my back, and stumbled off toward school.

As soon as the bell rang for the beginning of English class, Ms. Staats announced that she was collecting our stories and poems for *The Beacon*.

I felt pretty bad because not only was I not

handing in something for *The Beacon*, I hadn't been able to finish my regular homework either. As it was, I was going to have to do the rest of my homework during lunch.

At the end of English class, Ms. Staats asked me to stay for a minute. I felt so tired and sad that I didn't think about being nervous.

"Allison," she said, "I just wanted to ask you if everything is all right."

"Sure," I answered. "Everything is fine, Ms. Staats."

"Well, I noticed that you didn't hand anything in for *The Beacon*," she continued.

"I know," I said. "I'm sorry."

"And yesterday," she went on, "you didn't even finish the class assignment. And I've noticed that you've been acting and looking...well, different is the word, I guess. Are you sure everything is okay?"

I knew I couldn't say anything at all or I would start crying. I bit my lip, nodded, and then hurried out of the room. I rushed to my locker as fast as I could, afraid that if somebody talked to me I would cry. When I finally got there, the first person I saw was Randy. She was leaning against the wall across the hall from my locker. She was trying to look casual, but I could tell from the look on her face that something was up.

I took a couple of deep breaths to calm myself down, opened my locker, and started to put my books away, pretending that I hadn't seen her. What I really wanted to do was run across the hall and beg her to talk to me. But I didn't know how to put what I felt into words.

"Hey, Al," Randy said.

I just knew that I'd start crying if I looked at Randy's face. So I turned around slowly and stared at her shoes instead, trying hard not to show her how upset I was. She was wearing white sneakers, decorated with fluorescent pink and yellow flamingos and red and blue beach balls.

"Hello, Randy." I couldn't get my voice to work much louder than a whisper.

"Listen, I can't stay long, but I just had to ask you something. What's going on with you these days, huh? Did Charlie run you over with his bike or something? I mean, ever since the makeover, you've been acting really weird. And that business with Stacy and Eva and Laurel just wasn't like you at all. What's wrong?" Randy asked.

"Well, I —"

"Oh, come on, Allison. First you let Stacy and her friends pick on Sabrina. We had planned to talk about it at Sabs's house on Thursday, before we picked out a movie," said Randy as she stopped and looked at me. "But you didn't even call to tell us you couldn't make it. Ever since this modeling stuff started, you've been a different person."

Oh, no! I'd forgotten all about going to Sabrina's house on Thursday. I never had a chance to tell them about the second shoot at the Widmere Mall. No wonder they didn't want to talk to me.

"Is it Stacy?" Randy asked. "You model types want to hang together, is that it?"

How could Randy think that I liked Stacy Hansen more than I liked any of them? Ever since Stacy lied to me about Bruce, I had realized that she was really as awful as they had all said she was. I had to make Randy understand that everything was just a little crazy right now.

"Randy, about Stacy. . . I —"

"I don't want to talk about your *friend* Stacy, Allison Cloud," Randy said quietly. "I know that I'm right about her, but maybe — just maybe — I was wrong about you. *Ciao*, Al." Randy turned around and walked away. Something told me I should run after her and explain, but I felt as if my feet were stuck to the floor. I had never been so miserable in all my life.

Somehow I got through the rest of the day. It was awful. I had no one to eat lunch with, and no one was waiting for me by my locker after school. I wasn't even glad that it was the weekend.

On Saturday morning I got up and did every bit of homework I had. I even did the science homework that wasn't due until Tuesday. I tried to work on a poem for *The Beacon*, hoping that if it was too late this time I'd have something extra early for the next issue, but I couldn't think of anything to write. I didn't even feel like reading.

A couple of times I picked up the phone and started to call Randy, Katie, or Sabrina, but I always hung up. On Saturdays the four of us usually did something together. This Saturday seemed unbearable without my friends to talk to. What was I going to do? I didn't know how to tell them that this had all been a terrible misunderstanding, and that I had no intention of being Stacy's friend.

Finally, just when I couldn't stand being in my room anymore, my mother asked me to watch

Charlie while she went grocery shopping. So I joined Charlie outside. I admit it felt good to get out in the fresh air.

Charlie and I had a great time. We played Ghostbusters for a while and then we started playing with this neat science kit that my parents had bought him. When my mother got back from grocery shopping, I helped her unload the groceries from the car.

"I saw Katie, Sabrina, and Randy in town," my mother said. "I was surprised you hadn't asked to go with them. Is something going on with you girls?" I followed her inside with another bag and put it down on the kitchen counter. At that moment I just wanted to crawl into her lap like Charlie does when he's upset and pour the entire story out to her. What if she thought it was a good idea to become better friends with Stacy? You know, broaden my horizons and stuff like that. What if she didn't understand that I didn't think I wanted to grow up at all? It was too confusing. So I just said, "No, not really. I mean, well, sort of. Where were they, anyway?" I asked.

"They were waiting on a movie line."

I walked out onto the porch. I thought about Sabrina, Randy, and Katie sitting in the movie theater without me at that very moment, and I felt miserable. I looked around and saw my grandfather sitting in his favorite spot, smoking his pipe. It was nice to know that some things never changed.

I looked up. The sky was an incredible blue, and there were a few big, puffy clouds rolling by.

Suddenly my grandfather cleared his throat. I turned around to look at him.

"There is something that my grandmother used to tell me," he said, "and now I will tell it to you.

"It is a story," he began. "A caterpillar who crawled among his friends wished to be a butterfly. But when the creature grew wings and flew in the air, it was lonely for its life on the ground. One day it flew very low and landed on the tree stump where it once had lived. But the other caterpillars did not know what it was. They did not recognize their friend, so they ran away."

He stopped speaking and put his pipe back in his mouth. I didn't know what to say. I had no idea what he was talking about. But, as I sat there on the steps, I got to thinking. I guess when Sabs, Katie, Randy, and I all went to the Widmere Mall that first Saturday two weeks ago, we were all

like caterpillars who wanted to turn into butter-
flies. Then after I got to model for *Belle* it was as if
I had been changed into a butterfly — but no one
else had.

I thought about the way I had changed after
that first shoot at the football field. I had become
more fashion conscious. But I liked some of the
changes. They made me feel good about myself. I
realized that just because I had changed on the
outside didn't mean I had changed on the inside.
Suddenly I stood up. I knew what I had to do. It
was up to me to show them that I hadn't changed,
and that I was still the same old Allison.

I decided to walk into town to Fitzie's. Katie,
Randy, Sabrina, and I usually go there after a
movie and have a hamburger or something. I figured I would just wait for them and when they
showed up I would explain everything that had
been going on. They had to listen to me.

I went into Fitzie's, sat down at the counter,
and ordered a soda. The movie hadn't let out yet,
and even though there were a few families there
having lunch, it was pretty empty for Fitzie's. I
took out the notebook and pen I had brought with
me. While I was walking along, an idea had come
to me for a story to submit to *The Beacon*. It was

based on the story my grandfather had told me about the caterpillars and the butterfly.

I became lost in my writing until I heard Stacy's shrill voice. I turned my head and saw her sliding into her regular booth with Eva, B.Z., and Laurel.

"Gosh, I don't know why she's not here yet!" Stacy said.

"Did you let your mother know what time the movie was supposed to end?" Eva asked.

"Of course," Stacy answered.

"And she definitely said she would bring them to you here?" B.Z. asked.

"Yes. I told her to bring them here so we could all see them," Stacy said, looking around and catching my eye. She quickly turned back to her table. She acted as though she hadn't seen me, but I knew she had.

Just then the door opened and Katie walked in, followed by Sabrina and Randy.

"Well, I thought it was a really stupid movie," Randy said.

"Oh, Randy, didn't you think it was romantic?" Katie asked her.

"Mushy was more like it," Randy answered.

They went on talking, as they sat down at a

booth in the back. They hadn't noticed me yet, and I wasn't sure what to do. When I left my house it had all seemed simple, but now I was scared. What if they were so mad, they wouldn't even talk to me?

Suddenly Stacy jumped up from her table.

"There she is!" she said excitedly, rushing for the door.

I looked out the front window and saw Stacy's mother's car pulling up in front of Fitzie's. Then I saw Stacy run up to the car, take something from her mother, and hurry back.

"I've got it!" she announced as she came in the door. She held a gray folder above her head.

"These are magazine layouts from my photo session with *Belle Magazine*. Now, it was really hard for my mother to get this," said Stacy in a voice loud enough for everyone in Fitzie's to hear, "and we have to be really careful because I'm going to save them for my portfolio."

Stacy put the folder down on the table in front of her. She pulled out a few pages and held them up. Some people had left their tables and were gathering around her.

"What is going on here?!" Stacy shrieked. "There must be some sort of mistake." She grabbed the folder from the table and shook it. "There must be some pages missing!"

Eva picked up a page from the table and looked at it. "Stacy," she said, sounding a little annoyed, "I don't see you on this page."

"Hey, Stacy how come Allison's in every shot? I only see one picture of you in the whole thing!" B.Z. announced.

Someone in the crowd began to giggle. Slowly people returned to their tables.

"I should have known this would happen," Stacy said. "The whole thing was really an amateur operation. I only agreed to do it because they begged me to, you know."

I decided I had had just about enough of this. I stood up. "Stacy, that's not true, and you know it!" I said loudly.

Stacy looked at me in surprise. Then her face got red, and she yelled, "Allison Cloud, I would be embarrassed being in something like this if I were you. Anyway, *Belle* fashions are so immature!"

"It was good enough for you when you thought you were going to be in the pictures," I told her. "And if it was such an embarrassing thing to do, why did you force your mother to get hold of the layouts and bring them all the way down here to Fitzie's for you to show them off?!" I was suddenly aware that everyone in Fitzie's was staring at us, but I didn't care.

"What do you know about it, Allison?" Stacy screamed. "You never even knew how to put on makeup until you went to the *Belle* makeover. Now you think you're so great just because someone took a few pictures of you! And you were obviously lying to Bruce about Darla. *Belle* isn't taking you to New York to model. Talk about showing off!"

I walked toward Stacy. "As a matter of fact, Stacy, Darla did ask me to come to New York, but I don't think modeling is so great. I wouldn't go to New York for anything in the world! I think that anyone who thinks she's better than everyone else just because she has her picture in a magazine is a real jerk!"

"I don't have to listen to this — I'm leaving!" said Stacy, picking up her jacket and storming out of Fitzie's, leaving the pictures on the table.

Suddenly I realized that I was standing in the middle of Fitzie's and that everyone was looking at me — even Sabrina, Randy, and Katie. My knees were shaking but at the same time I felt as though a weight had been lifted off me.

"Way to go, Al!" Randy exclaimed, coming up to me. "You really told her!" she said, punching me lightly in the shoulder.

Katie rushed over. "Come on, Allison, we have a table over here," she said.

"I think Allison might like to see these," said Sabs, scooping up the pages of photographs from the table, "since she is the one in the pictures." Eva, Laurel, and B.Z. just sat there with their mouths hanging open.

"Oh, Allison," said Sabrina with a smile. "You were great!"

"No," I told her, "I wasn't great. As a matter of fact I've been pretty un-great lately, and I'm sorry."

Katie put her hand on my arm. "We're just glad you're back with us."

"Wow," Randy teased, "who is this glamorous person with all the hair? She must be famous!"

"May I have your autograph?" Sabrina asked.

"I just want your clothes!" Katie exclaimed, her head buried in the pages. We all laughed.

"I know. I know. I deserve it," I said. "I guess everything just got out of control."

"Well, we weren't very understanding either,"

Sabrina admitted.

"Yeah, we were pretty mean to you about Stacy," Katie said.

"No, you guys were right about her," I told them.

"Did they really want you to go to New York?" Sabs asked.

"Yeah, but I'm going to tell them to forget it."

Randy stared at me in disbelief. "You must be crazy!" she said.

"You sure are!" said Katie. "And we wouldn't have you any other way!"

"Just one question," said Sabrina.

"What?" I asked.

The three of them looked at each other, smiling.

"WHO IS BRUCE?!" they all said at once.

I laughed. "Oh, he's probably here in the pictures." Then I thought of something "That is, if you want to look at them."

"Are you kidding?" Sabs said. "Of course we want to see them!"

There was a huge picture of me dumping leaves on Bruce's head. There was the touch football game, but since they had cut off the edges of the picture, Stacy and Freddy weren't even in it. I could see why she was so mad. She had been cut out of just about every picture. There was one picture of all of us linking arms on the football field, but it was so tiny you could barely see our faces. I saw the picture of me holding up the dress for Suzi to see. My arm ached just looking at it.

And there was a close-up of me in the tortoise-shell glasses. Sabs said they looked pretty good on me. Katie said I ought to wear glasses more often, even if I didn't need them. Randy decided we should all go to Spex, the eyeglass place in the mall next weekend and try on fake glasses. It was great being back with my friends again. Modeling had been fun, especially meeting Bruce. I had learned a lot of new things, but I was through with the fashion business — at least for a while!

# Titles in the GIRL TALK series

**LOOK FOR THE GIRL TALK SERIES!**
*COMING SOON TO A STORE NEAR YOU!*

# TALK BACK!

TELL US WHAT YOU THINK ABOUT GIRL TALK

Name _____

Address _____

City _____ State _____ Zip _____

Birthday: Day _____ Mo _____ Year _____

Telephone Number (____) _____

1) On a scale of 1 (The Pits) to 5 (The Max), how would you rate Girl Talk?    Circle One:

    1    2    3    4    5

2) What do you like most about Girl Talk?

___Characters___Situations___Telephone Talk

Other _____

3) Who is your favorite character?   Circle One:

    Sabrina         Katie         Randy
    Allison         Stacy         Other

4) Who is your least favorite character?

_____

5) What do you want to read about in Girl Talk?

_____

_____

Send completed form to :
Western Publishing Company, Inc.
1220 Mound Avenue Mail Station #85
Racine, Wisconsin 53404

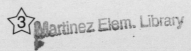